A surge of desperation made her call him back

"Max?"

He stopped but didn't turn, his spine stiffening slightly at her tone. "Yes?" he asked gruffly.

She saw the angry clenching of his jaw and sighed inwardly. "Nothing," she returned, and forced herself to sound lighter than she actually felt. "I was just wondering whether mistresses warranted goodbye kisses, that's all."

His conscience pricked, he spun to face her. "I've only just gotten out of bed after making mad, passionate love to you!" he snapped. "Surely you can't be feeling neglected already."

Max *thought* he made love, Clea considered when he'd gone. In fact all he did was indulge in his ability to give and take sensual pleasure. *She* made love. There was a world of difference.

MICHELLE REID lives in Cheshire, England, dividing her time between being a full-time housewife and mother looking after her husband and two teenage daughters and writing. She says her family takes it very well, fending for themselves until she "comes up for air," though she's not sure which they find harder to put up with, being cleaned and polished when she's in a housekeeping mood or being totally ignored when she's absorbed in writing and tends to forget they're alive! She has a passion for fresh air and exercise, which she gets at the local tennis club.

MICHELLE REID

a question of pride

Harlequin Books

TORONTO • NEW YORK • LONDON
AMSTERDAM • PARIS • SYDNEY • HAMBURG
STOCKHOLM • ATHENS • TOKYO • MILAN

Harlequin Presents first edition January 1989
ISBN 0-373-11140-1

Original hardcover edition published in 1988
by Mills & Boon Limited

CHAPTER ONE

DEEP purple eyes hid a lot as they watched the man who had so recently left the bed stroll back into the bedroom wearing only a towel, slung low on his hips. He had just taken a shower, and was rubbing at his hair with another towel, frowning, lost in thought.

'For God's sake, get up, Clea!' he muttered, deep-voiced and surly, his glance barely brushing her where she lay, still reluctant to leave the rumpled bed. 'It's late enough as it is!'

She yawned, stretching lazily, dragged herself up on an elbow, shook back the tumble of blue-black hair from her face, then returned to watching him move about the room, gathering together his scattered clothes.

A bit of a dark Adonis, was Max: all healthy tan and rippling muscle. His skin shone with health, his movements were deft and positive. Max was one of the world's high fliers. His successful Computer Electronics Company sent him all over the globe, touting for new business. He possessed a super-sharp mind to go with that super-charged, thirty-four-year-old body. Add to all of that the dark good looks any man would give his eye teeth for, and you had a man who knew how to play as successfully as he knew how to earn a comfortable crust.

Not the kind of man you would try to constrain inside a band of gold.

'Clea . . .!' The warning this time was terse with impatience.

'I can afford to lie in a bit today,' she said quietly, watching with mild interest for his reaction. 'My boss gave

5

me the morning off—in lieu of some heavy overtime recently.'

He missed the mockery in the little dig, but Clea wasn't surprised. He was only really concerned with getting to the office. The night was over, so the passionate man who had lain in her arms throughout the dark hours had been put away.

He paused in the process of pulling on his trousers, though, his attention caught by her at last. Blue eyes sought purple. 'I don't remember giving you any time off.' He was back pulling on the trousers, leaving them unfastened while he put on his shirt. 'Not for this morning, anyway . . . Damn!' he muttered, distracted again, searching the floor with impatient eyes. 'Why can't you remind me to hang up my clothes when I stay over here?'

I'm not your nanny, Max,' Clea said by way of another dig—it went wide of its target.

She spied one of his pale grey socks peeping out from a tangle of white bedding, and reached over to pull it free, handing it over to him in silence. He sat down on the edge of the bed and put it on, and the mattress depressed with his added weight, shifting Clea's relaxed body closer to his clean-smelling one, clothed now in a creased shirt and a sad-looking pair of trousers.

'You can't possibly have this morning off.' He had reverted to the former conversation because that was the one that affected the 'day-time Max', and it was day-time now. He found his other sock—and his tie by sheer good luck. Clea reached out to run a fingernail down his curved spine, her deep purple eyes twinkling when he shivered involuntarily to her touch. But he shrugged her off, not pausing in putting on his socks and shoes. 'We have the Stanwell contract to go over before I meet them for lunch. Be a good girl, darling,' he drawled with what would be the closest he would come to intimacy, now that he was up. 'Get up and get ready. You'll have to get to the office on time, since I'll have to go back to my flat to change.'

Clea let her head slide off her arm, back on to the pillows, her gaze still following his movements as he stood up to fasten his shirt and put on his tie, tying the knot with his square chin thrust high.

'I'm serious, Max,' she said. 'I won't be in this morning . . . I did warn you last week . . .' An outright lie, she had told him nothing of the sort, but Max wouldn't remember; he took in little that she said of a personal nature while they played their 'boss-secretary' roles. 'I've made arrangements to meet someone—an old schoolfriend—someone I can't put off.'

He was deciding whether to come the heavy and order her into work, combing his quickly drying hair with delicate flicks of his comb, leaning back at the knees so he could see in her dressing-table mirror, eyes revealing his contemplation.

'What time can I expect you in, then?' he asked her at last, and Clea's smile was wry. He'd decided against arguing the point with her because it was late and his time was precious. He had weighed up the pros and cons, and decided it was better to do without his secretary for a morning than delay his day any further.

'Mmm—oneish, I should think.'

'See you at one, then—no, I won't,' he amended as he pulled on his suit jacket and made for the bedroom door. 'I'll be out until two myself. I'll have to get Mandy to cover for you . . .' He was really muttering all this to himself, lost in the pending matters of the day. Clea was all but forgotton.

'Mandy already knows,' she informed him drily. He should have known that Clea was nothing if not efficient.

'Max . . .?' A sudden surge of desperation made her call him back.

He stopped but didn't turn, his spine stiffening slightly at the tone in her voice. 'Yes?' he enquired gruffly.

She saw the angry clenching of his jaw and sighed inwardly. 'Nothing,' she returned, and forced herself to sound lighter than she actually felt. 'I was just wondering if mistresses warranted goodbye kisses, that's all.'

That must have pricked at his conscience a little, because he spun around to face her. 'Good God, Clea!' he sighed. 'I've only just fallen out of that bed after making mad passionate love to you! Surely you can't be feeling neglected already!'

She stretched again, pretending to yawn behind a hand, looking unconsciously beautiful—all gypsy seduction, with her cloud of blue-black hair a shimmering tumble around her. Max tightened his grip on the doorhandle.

'No, I don't feel neglected,' she assured him quietly. Just very unloved. 'See you later, hmm?'

He sent her a quick smile, one of those blinding ones that always took her breath away. Then he was striding out of the room and out of her flat, leaving Clea staring at the ceiling, alone.

Max thought he *made love*, when what he actually did was indulge in his ability to give and enjoy immense sensual pleasure. *She* made love to him. There was a world of difference.

He was a loner, a free spirit. He had no ties and wanted none. His loyalty was one hundred per cent dedicated to his company. He was a regular thunderball of energy. He could set women's teeth on edge just to look at him. He was single and wealthy, and liked being that way. He made love—no, she corrected that—he 'enjoyed sex' with that same single-minded desire for perfection that he applied to his work. To be fair to him, when he gave, he gave totally—if only temporarily.

He liked to keep these two sections of his life completely separate. Yet for some reason he had broken this rule when he'd turned to Clea for a lover, and he didn't much like the situation, either. She knew that, because he was so very careful not to let anyone at the office know about their affair. Joe knew, but then Joe was not just Max's personnel manager, he was also his closest friend. And Joe was shrewd; it would be difficult to hide anything from him, for he possessed an invisible antenna that could read people's thought-patterns at fifty paces.

But, other than Joe, Max was super-careful. He reacted to Clea being both his lover and his private secretary as a married man would to hide his adultery. During the day, Clea was the very cool and efficient secretary doing his fetching and carrying, typing his letters and taking his phone calls. But, once darkness fell and the office door closed behind them, she became his woman, his seducer, the one to put the flame in his cool blue eyes. Three, maybe four times a week, they would meet, dine at some intimate restaurant and maybe dance a little on some small, dimly lit dance-floor before they would come back here, to her flat, to spend long, passionate hours locked in each other's arms.

In the morning, Max would revert back to the businessman as soon as his feet hit the floor. He never offered her a lift to work after one of his overnight stops, even though his car was parked at her kerbside and she would have to leave at the same time as he to get to work. But Clea didn't really mind. She, like Max, preferred their relationship to remain a secret from their fellow workers, for she had no desire to become the nub of everyone else's gossip. Max liked everything to be tidy, with no hassle. If Clea ever tried to rock the boat she would be out on her ear, she had no doubts about that.

She could get up now he'd gone, and she slid her feet to the floor and slowly sat up, her expression haunted.

It was drawing to an end. Five months of bliss, of contrary heartache—soon, it would all be over, through no one's fault but her own. But knowing and accepting that didn't make it any easier to bear.

Oh, God! On a choking sob, Clea got up and ran for the bathroom, slamming the door shut behind her and locking herself in.

Eleven-thirty that morning found Clea sitting alone in a café, staring into the congealed remains of a cup of too creamy coffee.

She was pregnant.

She had suspected it for a while now, but the doctor had only just confirmed it . . . And she was pregnant.

The girl behind the café counter had a transistor radio on low. A sad love song was playing—Elaine Paige and Barbara Dickson singing about how good it was—how fine! But they couldn't understand, when they'd known from the beginning how it would end, why they were now falling apart. Clea could tell them, she knew from experience. It was that cruel emotion 'hope' that was to blame.

She had *hoped* to be the exception to the rule—the one Max would come to love enough to marry. But he hadn't and he wouldn't. Hadn't he made it crystal-clear from the start that theirs was an affair only, that he had no room in his life for any heavy commitment? And hadn't she accepted all his provisos when she had let him become her lover?

Fool, Clea!

It was entirely her own fault that she was pregnant. She had taken on the responsibility of protecting them against this happening, and she must now bear the consequences of failing Max in this one area he had trusted her with.

She was going to have to work out what she was going to do, because when Max found out he was going to be furious. In fact, she realised at that precise moment, she couldn't let him find out, at least, not until she'd formulated some plan, organised herself to an extent where his knowing wouldn't alter things. She wouldn't, *couldn't* marry him under these unhappy circumstances—and he would suggest marriage. Max was an honourable man, in his own way. But, while marrying her, he would hate her for it.

She was going to have to end their relationship, and quickly. She hadn't dared get out of bed this morning while he was still there because for the last few days she had been sick in the morning. She had managed to hide it from him so far, but not for much longer . . .

'You all right, dear?'

Clea looked up to find the café assistant standing over her, her heavily made-up face concerned. She smiled to reassure her, but it wasn't a very convincing smile, and the woman seemed to understand because she gave Clea's shoulder a sympathetic pat and moved away without another word.

It was time to go. Clea got up and gathered her things together. She knew she must be pale because she *felt* pale. It was difficult to do anything about it while she was so numb inside. It was silly, trying to sort through her muddled thoughts while she felt like this; tonight would be soon enough to think—and really begin the worrying. Max wasn't seeing her tonight, he had a business dinner to go to. She would go home after work, lock herself away inside her flat and think then—think clear and hard.

Clea was working at her desk when Max shot back into the office like a tornado, striding past her desk without even offering her a glance.

'Switch me an outside line through,' he commanded, then disappeared into his own office, closing the door behind him.

She let out a long breath, unaware that she had been holding it until it came from her tensed lungs with a whoosh. Guilt and fear? Something like that, she realised heavily. She had been afraid Max would take one look at her and know, when in actual fact he hadn't even glanced at her.

Not that that was unusual, she acknowledged as she gave him his open line by flicking a switch on her communications console beside her elbow. Max was behaving as he always did here; it was she who had changed since they'd parted this morning. She sat back, eyes clouding, with an expression of sad indulgence. He had always been curt, demanding, full of ceaseless energy . . .

He must have got the Stanwell contract. He would be ringing around now, warning his sub-contractors to expect large orders for components. He liked to do this initial sounding-out personally, because it made them sit up and take notice; then he would delegate around his minions to leave himself free to hunt for more work.

He buzzed her, and she jumped, startled out of her inactivity.

'Yes, Max?'

'Bring yourself in here, will you?' Snap, the line went dead.

Clea took a deep breath, hoped the tension she was experiencing inside didn't show too much on her pale face, picked up her pad and pencil and went into his office.

He had changed his clothes—as he had said he would have to do. Clea moved quietly across the room and sat down opposite him. The dark pin-striped suit looked good on him; it gave that lean, muscled frame of his some added impact. The white shirt made his skin look darker, his neat grooming a confirmation of the way he ran his life, all neat and tidy, all straight lines with the unforeseen catered for.

I'm carrying your child, Max, she told him silently. I'm going to have your baby.

Tears smarted the backs of her eyes and she had to blink them away. Shock, she realised, staring pale-faced down at her knees, where her notepad lay on the soft wool cloth of her black office suit.

'Did you meet your friend?'

'What——?' She had thought him engrossed in the sheaf of papers stacked in front of him, so his voice when he spoke startled her again. Steady! She warned herself, you're in danger of falling apart—just like the song on the café radio said she would. 'Yes. We went to that little bistro place off Regent Square.'

Max wasn't listening. She could tell by the way his eyes whipped over the closely typed print on the pages in front of him. He had only asked out of courtesy. He wasn't really interested in anything she did, unless it took place between the sheets . . .

Cynicism, Clea, she accused herself bitterly. Not like you at all. Here you are, lying to him, loving him and hating him all at the same time, and the sad part about it is that Max has no idea!

'Ready now?' He looked up, his eyes narrowing suddenly as he caught her pained expression. Then he blinked to dismiss the vague idea that she wasn't the girl he was used to seeing at this time of the day. 'Six copies,' he murmured, sliding several documents over the desk towards her. 'To go to . . .' And the afternoon began.

It was five o'clock before either of them came up for air. They had worked quietly and effectively together throughout the afternoon. The pace of work and Max's usual dynamism had helped Clea to forget her personal problems, but the paleness must still have been there in her soft ivory skin, because Max paused by her desk as he came out of his office. She guessed that he was seeing her clearly for the first time now that the hectic day was drawing to a close.

'Clea, are you feeling OK?' He leaned his knuckles on her desk, dipping his dark head a little to see her face better.

If she had been in the right frame of mind, she would have appreciated his concern. Instead, she pinned a smile on her face and lifted her head to show it to him. 'I'm fine,' she lied, and forced the smile wider to prove the point. 'Just one of those days, I think . . . I'll be glad to get home tonight and put my feet up.'

He was frowning in usual 'Max' style, his blue eyes dark with the glimmer of affection, and her heart squeezed—going out to him, because she loved him, and this warmer Max was the one she couldn't help responding to.

'Beautiful Clea,' he murmured deeply, then took her by surprise by reaching out to gently touch her cheek. 'Beautiful—beautiful Clea, I think I'm . . .' He stopped himself, fingertips tensing against her skin just before he snatched them away, straightening, his expression odd—shocked, almost.

Tension seemed to leap up from nowhere, and Clea felt puzzled. What had he been about to say that had brought him up short like that? She felt a burst of panic—he couldn't know, could he? He couldn't have guessed? No, of course he hadn't.

Max was giving himself a mental shake. She actually saw it happen, although he showed no physical signs of doing so, and his smile held its normal teasing quality. Gone was the look of intensity.

Clea's own lack of self-awareness meant she had no idea

what Max actually saw when he looked at her. The 'beautiful, exotic gypsy', as he liked to teasingly call her, was not far from the truth. Jet-black, curling hair pulled into soft, lively waves by the sheer weight and length of it meant that she had to keep it severely confined when at work and, though Max adored her hair when it was loose and wildly free, worn in its tight knot, it only helped to accentuate the perfect oval of her face and her ivory smooth skin. Her eyes were large and dark, their colour a fascinating mixture of lavender and midnight-blue depending on her mood, and they tilted slightly at the outer corners to add a little mystery to the gypsy quality in her. Her nose was small and straight, her mouth generous, sensually so. She was tall and slender, but beautifully curved. Clea had the ability to stir the male senses without even being aware of doing it. She did that to Max every time he looked at her, and that made him angry. He didn't like the vulnerability it revealed in his implacable character.

'Have you nearly finished?' He glanced at his watch, obviously eager to get off.

'Ten more minutes, that's all,' she assured him. Remembering his dinner date tonight, she gave him a reassuring smile—Max didn't like to think that she was working late when he wasn't. He was a conscientious enough boss to think it unfair to expect his staff to do more than he was prepared to do himself. 'Have a nice evening,' she added as a final push for him.

'I'll pick you up tomorrow night.' He seemed reluctant to go now, his stance hesitant—restless. Tomorrow was a Saturday, and they were going to the theatre. Clea had booked the tickets herself earlier in the week, to see the latest Tim Rice musical. The song that had been haunting her all day came from it. 'We could go on to a club later if you wish . . . have some supper—maybe dance a little?'

What was the matter with him? Clea felt confused by this unusual show of hesitance.

'Are you sure you're all right?' He must be feeling confused, too, to ask the same question twice, she noted wryly. Max wasn't the type to repeat himself. Maybe some of her distress was showing, and Max was unconsciously picking up on it.

Nerves made her resort to mockery. 'What in heaven's name could be wrong with me, Max? You'll have me wondering if you're suffering from a guilty conscience if you keep this up!' They never shared this kind of conversation here in the office.

He didn't like that; it stiffened his spine, his face hardening. 'Anyone would think I'm cruel to you, to hear you,' he muttered and turned to stride angrily for the door.

Clea looked miserably down at her typewriter. 'Sometimes you are,' she replied heavily. 'As you and I both know.'

She went back to her typing, tapping away furiously, while Max stood by the open door, watching her. He wanted to say something, defend himself. He was angry—taken aback by her sudden attack on him. It happened so rarely that, when it did, he didn't know how to handle it. He glanced at his watch, then back at Clea's bowed head. The tension around them sharpened to an unbearable point, then Max sighed impatiently and left the room without saying another word.

Clea stopped typing and pulled the piece of paper out of the machine. She had written gibberish, unadulterated gibberish.

CHAPTER TWO

CLEA sat for a full five minutes staring at the wall opposite, seeing nothing. Outside, the sounds of the usual mass evacuation that took place every evening around this time went on without her being conscious of it. She felt cut off, isolated by the weight of her problems.

They began crowding in on her, dragging her down into a deep depression. Distress made a fluttering attempt at taking hold of her, and she stood up abruptly, her chair scraping on its castors, echoing shrilly in the too quiet office.

She then did something she had never done before. She went into Max's office, closed the door behind her, made for the walnut cabinet where he kept his private stock of spirits and poured herself a neat whisky. She took it with her over to the big window, sipping shakily at the drink, to look down on a busy London beneath her. The rush hour was in full swing and, though she was too high up to hear any of the noises that went with that Friday night rush, she could see the way traffic had already come to a near standstill, how the crush of human bodies rushed along like armies of busy ants.

The executive offices of the Computer Electronics Company took up the whole of the top floor of the six-storey building. Max owned the lot. Each floor was taken up with some specialised computer process or another, design, electronics, data process. The huge typing pool, where she had originated from before ending up up here as his secretary. It all went on beneath them, the finished product being belched out on the ground floor where Max would go to inspect, run and re-run his latest creation until he could use it as well as his highly paid experts. Then his garrison of salesmen would go out to sell the product, while Max concentrated on bigger things. It was he who landed the more lucrative contracts—the computers designed for tailor-made functions. It was he who kept the company moving for ever upwards. He was its jugular, its heart, its life and soul. Without his driving force behind it, the company would collapse . . . as she felt *she* was about to do now.

It had all begun so innocently. She had been nothing but a very junior secretary, working on the second floor as a 'floater' for the troop of salesmen to use when they needed her. She had only ever seen Max once in those first six months that she worked for him, and then it had been from a distance, when he'd made one of his very rare visits to the typing pool. He had paused by the glass partition, outside in the corridor, his dark face peering in at the two long lines of busy word processors where girls of all ages, shapes and sizes sat working. She had noticed him looking in, because at that moment she had been walking towards the paned glass that partitioned the main corridor from the large typing pool. Their eyes had caught and held for a split second—a second in which she learned the meaning of all the drooling the other girls did over their elusive boss. She'd received an impression of black hair, black frowning brows and a pair of piercing blue eyes that had rendered her breathless. They had also stopped her in her tracks, pinning her to the spot while he, in his arrogance, had inspected her from head to tingling toes.

She'd been so young, she realised now when it was too late. Too young for a man as worldly-wise as Max. He'd packed too much living into the fourteen years separating them for it to be a sensible thing for her to get involved with him.

It had been he who had broken the eye-to-eye contact that day, he who had lifted the corner of his mouth in that mocking smile he liked to use to make people feel ill at ease, and it had been *she* who had been left there feeling foolish, her face hot with colour. The rest of the girls had stared at her as though she'd just physically attacked their beloved boss. They had teased her about the incident for days afterwards. But, as the weeks went by, and they were not treated to any more visitations from the revered employer, life settled back to its normal humdrum calm and all was forgotten. Until Max's secretary left to emigrate to Canada with her new husband, and Clea was offered the job.

She had been barely twenty, and as naïve as they came then. Not so now, she realised wryly. It was amazing what one could learn within a few months of Max's influence. She had gone from a girl—who saw a man only as someone to enjoy a pleasant evening with before she left him at her flat door with a thank-you peck on the cheek—to a woman, in every sense of the word. A cool, very controlled, sophisticated lady who had learned how to temper her emotions to suit the man she loved.

She had worked for him for a month before Max asked her out. And then it had been a classic case of the boss asking the secretary to work late, then offering her dinner to recompense. The next time, the dinner was offered without any back-up excuse.

He was attractive, breathtakingly sophisticated, and possessed a charm—when he decided to turn it on—that was all but impossible to combat. In fact, she thought now as she looked back on that time, Max had turned her head without even having to work at it much. He didn't even bother to wrap his proposition up in fancy words. He just told her, over dinner one evening, that he wanted to be her lover, then waited casually for her reply.

She found some comfort now in remembering that she'd had the strength to turn him down that first time. But his answering laugh had been mocking, as if he had been sure of his own power over her. He had known, even while she was refusing him in her cool, off-handed way, that he would win in the end.

He'd discovered her innocence only when it was too late to draw back. She had been too shy to tell him, and yes, too afraid of losing him if she did tell him. He had been furious at first, then rather pleased; then so smug that it had been aggravating.

'I've never made love to a virgin before,' he'd whispered, then set about teaching her all he knew, making her into the woman he'd wanted her to be, conditioning her until the shy young girl was gone for ever. And she'd let him, because she loved him, and she'd known, even then, that her complete acquiescence to his wants was the only way she would keep him.

He might not love her in return, but he made her feel beautiful and infinitely desirable. And sometimes his loving would move on to a plane beyond the physical norm. He would worship her, pay homage to every single inch of her, until she could only lie boneless, barely breathing amid the clouds of sensation he was arousing in her. It was at these times that she could convince herself that he loved her, because in the giving of so much Max would become lost himself. Their bodies moved to a rhythm of their own creation, and he would tremble, that big, dark being who so enveloped her, he would tremble in her arms and *be* hers, for those few precious moments, completely hers. It would shake him, though. Max never liked what overtook him at those times, and in the aftermath he would grow morose—angry, almost. He never remarked on it, but she knew; he hated losing control to such a degree, because in doing so he was revealing a desperate need for her. Clea had a suspicion that Max had rarely—if ever—experienced such a depth of emotion with any other woman, and it frightened him, made him feel threatened by what could develop between them. After a night like that he would draw back a little, become remote and unreachable and maybe not come near her for days.

Last night had been one of those times. That was what made his gesture in her office earlier all the more confusing, because he had come forwards when usually he would be backing off. He had acted very much out of character, and it confused her—bothered her at a time when she was confused and bothered enough.

It was dark outside now, the street lights turning everything a dull gold colour. Hardly anyone seemed to be moving down on the ground now, and once again the feeling of being very much alone assailed her. She took a deep gulp at the whisky, then grimaced at the bitter taste. She didn't even like the stuff, yet she had felt the need for some kind of bolster—still did, for her nerves were screaming for release. Pain, fear, depression, and a thousand other emotions were vying for domination, while she stood, as outwardly calm as she always appeared.

Thank God for self-control! Clea mocked herself bitterly, then scorned herself for the self-deception. She wasn't in control, she was in shock.

A pale hand drifted to the flat of her stomach, and Clea looked down at it, her slender fingers spread out across the dark cloth of her tailored skirt. How long would she remain like this—slim, neat-figured? Not long; she was already in her second month of pregnancy. Her condition would begin to show soon.

Max had planted a seed inside her, and it was going to grow into a baby, a beautiful, dark-haired, blue-eyed baby. She trembled at the sudden and unexpected jolt of emotion that gave her. A baby . . . hers and Max's baby . . . Abortion was out! she decided, with a fierceness that yet again surprised her.

Marriage to Max was out. She took another gulp of whisky.

And her job. That was going to have to go. She couldn't stay here now, not without losing her pride. Max would hate it if he had to see her every day, growing big with his child, her figure—the body that was all that kept him coming back to her—becoming distorted and unattractive. No, she couldn't remain working here.

She would have to go and see Joe, and plead with him to release her from her contract of employment without letting Max know. She would have to sever all reliance on Max before she told him why, or he would insist on keeping her on here, if only out of a sense of duty to her. She couldn't stand that. She couldn't stand the humiliation, working here and seeing him day after day, knowing that they would never again share a look, a tender touch . . .

Stop it!

Clea swung away from the window, angry with the way her rambling thoughts had gone. 'Drinking alcohol won't help much, either,' she rebuked herself out loud. 'Neither your mood, nor the baby you're carrying.' She walked into Max's cloakroom and poured the remains of her drink into the wash-basin, then rinsed out the glass, taking it back to the drinks cabinet and replacing everything as it should be.

'Go home, Clea,' she ordered herself.

But she didn't make any move towards the door:

instead, she made for the deep alcove where Max had two large leather chesterfield couches arranged by a low walnut table and several elegant green planters. She sat down wearily on one of the couches, leaning her dark head back and closing her eyes.

How was she going to manage? She had her flat, of course. It was hers, bought and paid for while her father had been alive. It had been the family home, then—and a happy one. She smiled at the memories conjured up in the quietness of Max's office. Her father was half-Italian. He had run his own very exclusive restaurant in London until he'd become ill. Then the business had had to be sold, because he could no longer look after it. When he'd died, he'd left her mother and herself financially secure. No debts, their own home to live in for as long as they wanted. But none of this was any compensation to the wife and child he'd left behind. Clea had worried for a time that her mother would never recover from her grief.

That had taken five years to fade. Then, just twelve months ago, she'd married James Laverne. He'd literally swept the fragile Amy off her feet. Again Clea smiled at the memory. Poor Amy had had no chance! James had seen her and simply tumbled into love! His pursuit of her mother had been intensive—and amusing. They had a lovely home in Shepperton now—a cosy love-nest that anyone would envy.

Amy had only been eighteen years old when she'd had Clea. She'd married the tall, dark and strikingly handsome Paolo Maddon against the wishes of her parents, at the very young age of seventeen, then went about proving all their premonitions of disaster wrong by remaining devoted to her husband beyond his death. And Paolo had been equally devoted to her. Amy was a tiny honey-blonde creature, with an air of defencelessness about her that went more than skin deep. She needed taking care of, for she was the dependent type by nature, and the five years she had spent without her first husband had probably been the worst ones of poor Amy's life. Now she had James to love and take care of her. And it was nice; Clea always felt a warm feeling inside when she thought of her mother and James, for their devotion to each other was just as strong as that between her father and Amy . . .

When James and Amy had married, they'd insisted Clea keep the flat as her own. 'You must have it, dear,' Amy had insisted when Clea had argued. 'I don't need the money we would get by selling, and your father would want you to live here. He loved this flat,' she said on a soft sigh. That dark Italian man would never fade from her mother's most tender thoughts—even the ultra-possessive James acknowledged that. 'We spent many wonderful years here. You have it,' she insisted again. 'Then I won't feel so guilty for deserting you.'

It had been the master stroke that had won Clea over. Amy might be delicate by nature but she wasn't stupid. She gave Clea no room to refuse. Now she was grateful for that humble surrender, for having the flat as her own was going to make things a lot easier for her in the future months . . . Her old bedroom would make an ideal nursery . . .

God! Her heart reeled. Pain, fear and excitement all culminated to form a mass of conflict inside her, and she dragged herself up off the couch, determined this time to go home to do her thinking.

Max's desk stood with its shiny top clear of paperwork. She walked slowly over to it, running her fingertips over the smooth wood. He always left his desk completely clear like this . . . Again his desire for neat and tidiness showed. A place for everything and everything in its place.

Clea sighed and turned towards the door as the ache inside her became unbearable.

Money . . . She considered this as she closed the door to Max's office and went about tidying her own desk. Her salary here had been exceptional, but she'd fallen into the habit of spending rather a lot on clothes since she'd met Max. It had all been a front she'd put up for his benefit. Max liked his women to look chic, elegant—like himself.

He wouldn't like her all blown up and looking like a balloon; she wasn't that sure that she fancied it much herself, wearing clothes that resembled tents, and trying to keep cool during those hot summer months and the final stage of her pregnancy.

October.

He—she—it—*he*, it was easier to think of the baby as a *he*. He would have to be dark-haired—how else could it be with two such dark-haired parents? If her mother couldn't manage to inject any of her fairness into Clea, then this poor soul had little chance of receiving any of his grandmother's fairer beauty.

She had her mother's eyes, though, Clea mused. Big lavender-blue eyes on a baby boy with Max's strong, sturdy build . . .

On a muffled sob, Clea grabbed up her coat and bag and rushed for the door.

The phone began ringing as she was preparing herself something to eat. Clea clutched at the sink, closing her eyes tightly and willing the jangling noise to stop. It would be her mother, calling for their weekly chat, as was her habit.

She didn't want to speak to Amy just now. She didn't want to speak to anyone—but her mother even less. She would have to sound happy, normal, and she felt neither. She would have to lie; she was finding herself doing that a lot recently. Amy would ask how she was, and she would have to say she was feeling fine, when in fact she felt lousy—absolutely lousy.

It was reaction, she told herself, as the telephone went on ringing and her nerve-ends began jangling along with the harsh noise. She was experiencing the reaction she had tried to hold at bay all day. She was aching with it, her heart pumping at a pounding pace.

'Shut up!' she gritted between clenched teeth. Her knuckles were white where she was gripping the sink. She was shivering, icy cold with it, a clammy sweat breaking out on her brow before springing out to drench her whole body. 'I'm not in!' she moaned achingly. 'I'm not in, Mother!'

Trust.

The word leaped like some leering apparition in front of her closed eyelids. Her mother *trusted* her daughter to behave morally. Clea *didn't trust* Max to be faithful—even to a lover. Max *trusted* her to guard against an unwanted pregnancy. She had failed her mother, she had failed Max. He had failed no one—because he had never requested her trust.

The telephone stopped.

Clea wilted heavily against the sink, her legs like jelly beneath her. The silence was a relief—sheer, utter relief—and she stayed as she was for a few moments, absorbing the peace, allowing her nerves time to settle again.

The half-prepared meal was thrown away in favour of a bath. Clea soaked herself for ages, not thinking, not feeling, just making her mind a complete blank and allowing the silence to enfold her like a blanket of empty comfort.

White-faced, despite the bath, Clea wrapped herself in her old red dressing-gown and padded through to her sitting-room. She had changed little in here since her mother had left. The room still held all the old knickknacks that made it home. A framed photograph of her with her parents, all looking at each other with love. The Axminster carpet that had been there for as long as she could remember. The Dralon three-piece suite, with its chunky loose cushions filled with soft swansdown. She should have gained some sort of comfort from the room, but she didn't, because the Clea of the times this room projected would not have got herself into this mess. She would never have risked hurting her parents in this way.

Damn Max!

She curled up in a chair, huddling into the warm robe as though the winter night had penetrated the room, when in fact the flat was centrally heated and quite warm. Her hair fell around her face and shoulders in a cloud of midnight-blue, enhancing her oval face and the paleness of her skin—an unnatural paleness for the usually vibrant Clea. Her mouth, too, was showing the signs of immense strain. Gone was the natural red fullness that gave away her deep, sensual nature. Instead, her lips were drawn tight and colourless. If Max saw her now he would be shocked by the change in her in just a few short hours.

Max . . . She had a whole weekend to get through with Max before she could begin to do anything about her situation. She could put him off, of course, but she didn't want to. She wanted this last weekend with him—needed it, in fact.

The telephone began ringing again, and she dived out of the chair to snatch up the receiver because she couldn't stand to listen to it ringing out a second time.

'Yes?' she snapped.

'Clea? Where have you been? I rang earlier but there was no reply . . .'

So, it was Max, not her mother who had rung. 'I was in the bath,' she lied, gripping tightly at the receiver.

'Oh.' Silence, an awkward silence that puzzled her.

Then, 'Are you alone?'

Clea leaned wearily against the wall behind her, wondering dully what he was getting at. He didn't usually call her up when they had their arrangements already made, and for some reason this diversion from his norm rankled her.

'No,' she lied again, finding it easier each time. 'I have a man waiting for me, you happen to be disturbing us.' Of course she was alone! she scorned silently. Wasn't she always alone without him?

'Don't tease, Clea.' His voice was pitched low and husky, creating within her a desperate need to see him, touch him. 'I was worried about you. I've been worrying about you all evening. Are you sure you're OK?'

She took in a steadying breath, sucking her lips back against her teeth to stop herself from saying something she would regret, from blurting out the whole sad mess to him. 'I'm fine . . . really, Max,' she assured him when she could trust herself to speak. 'Just tired. I was on my way to bed.'

Another silence, a strange, loaded silence that she couldn't decipher. What was the matter with him? Could he be drunk? It would be a first if he was. Max knew his own limits.

'Can I come?'

Clea stared blankly at the phone. Never—never had she heard him sound like this! Never had he called her up to invite himself around like this.

'What is this, Max?' she enquired suspiciously. 'Aren't you supposed to be hosting a business dinner? It's only——' she glanced at the gold carriage clock sitting on the mantel '—nine-thirty. You can't possibly have wrapped things up this early.'

She could almost see him shifting uncomfortably where he stood. It was certainly novel, Max feeling uncertain.

'It—it didn't work out,' she heard him mutter.

'What——what didn't work out?'

'The dinner. Look, for God's sake, Clea—I need you!' he bit out, rushing through the words. Angry—with himself, she guessed. If what he was saying was the truth, then he wouldn't be enjoying the feeling. 'I—I've needed you all damned day! I'm coming around now. I want to——'

'No.' She cut in on him tersely, and felt his surprise ricochet down the line. 'I'm tired,' she elaborated coldly. 'And I planned on a early night . . . I'll see you tomorrow.'

The receiver went down with a crash—before Max had a chance to argue with her. She couldn't cope—not tonight. She just couldn't.

CHAPTER THREE

SOMEONE was leaning on the doorbell. Clea swam up from a heavy sleep to register the familiar but unwanted sound. She groped blindly for the bedside-lamp switch, drenching the room in painful light, peering at her alarm clock. Ten o'clock—the earliness of the hour surprised her. She must have fallen into heavy sleep the moment her head had hit the pillow.

The shrill noise continued throughout her struggles out of her warm bed and into her dressing-gown. Whoever it was, there was a grim determination about the way they kept the bell ringing! She padded into the hall, wincing a protest at the din. The safety chain was on. She opened the door the few inches the chain allowed, and peered, sleepy-eyed, through the gap.

Max stood there, leaning against the doorframe, his hands pushed into the trouser pockets of his black evening suit. His bow-tie had been discarded, and the top few buttons of his dress-shirt had been tugged open to reveal some of the dark, taut skin beneath. His face was grim. There was a tense pause while they stared silently at each other, then, still without a word, Clea closed the door to remove the chain and stepped back to let him enter, her gaze lowered from his.

He came in slowly, slouching past her to take the door from her hand and close it quietly behind him.

'I w-was asleep.' She ran an unsteady hand through her tumbled hair.

Silence.

Clea swallowed thickly to remove the uncomfortable

30

lump from her throat. She was feeling a trifle woozy, which didn't help the situation, and she knew her eyes must look red and puffy because they *felt* that way. She felt a wreck—and in no way fit to deal with an angry Max.

He, on the other hand, looked magnificent, his hard, handsome face unfairly alluring. Her heart gave a painful squeeze. Would he always have this kind of effect on her? she wondered. This heady kind of excitement, tinged with the desolation of self-inadequacy?

'What's the matter, Clea?' he enquired softly, when it seemed like the silence would shatter into a million screams of pain around her.

She lifted her unhappy gaze to his, to find him studying her with those long, thick lashes of his shrouding his eyes. He wasn't angry, as she'd thought him to be. He actually looked concerned, and for some reason that made her feel more depressed. She had no answer to give him, and her head simply dipped again so that she didn't have to look at him.

'You look pale and miserable,' he observed gently, when no reply was forthcoming. 'You were strange this morning when I left here, you were the same at work . . . and quiet. I know I'm a self-centered swine most of the time,' he added on a heavy sigh, when she still made no sound, 'but I'm not so bad that I couldn't sense a difference in you . . . Can't you tell me what's wrong?'

Clea quivered on an inward sob. He sounded so gentle, and infinitely caring, and she so wanted to throw her arms around him, lose herself in the warm strength of him—take the comfort she knew he was offering her . . . She so wanted him to love her!

Tears stung at her eyes, and she was glad of the long fall of her hair that hid her face from his probing gaze. It was dark in the small hallway; only the spill of light from her bedroom lit their two grim forms.

'Is it me?' he asked huskily. 'Have I done or said something to upset you? Clea—what *is* it?' Impatience tinged his voice. He hadn't attempted to touch her. He just stood there—two feet away from her, with those sharp eyes of his pinned on her downturned face, waiting for some explanation for her odd behaviour.

She was trembling inside; in a moment, she would be trembling on the outside, too. His coming here at this time of night and without her expecting him to, had not given her time to gather herself, but she did so now, heaving in a deep breath and lifting her face to show him a reassuring expression.

'I'm just very tired, Max,' she told him quietly. 'You've done nothing—nothing at all.' Her voice sounded strange to her own ears: dead—was she dead? No, she was hurting too much inside to be dead. Life didn't give one such easy ways out.

Max looked grave, his stance full of tension. He was puzzled by her behaviour and feeling vaguely uncomfortable. Max didn't like to feel uncomfortable, he liked everything in his life to run on well oiled wheels.

'W-we females get like this sometimes, you know,' she offered wryly, her smile deliberately self-mocking. 'It's all in the hormones.'

'Ah!' He liked that. It was something he could understand. It removed the puzzlement—the discomfort.

Bitterly, she watched the tension leave him; his expression became easy, relaxing again into its usual lazy arrogance. When he reached out to draw her to him, Clea went willingly. She needed this. He might be offering her comfort for the wrong reasons, but she was feeling weak enough to accept whatever crumbs he wanted to throw her way. She loved him, and she was having his baby, and she was frightened of what the future held for her—a future without Max, without the small amount of affection he deigned to give her.

'I'm an insensitive cad!' He rebuked himself with enough humour in his tone to make her laugh which, she guessed, was what he intended her to do. His cheek came down to rub gently against hers. He smelled of *Dior*—that delicious elusive *Max* smell she associated only with him, because it was the only form of male cologne he ever used. Her arms crept around his lean waist, slender fingers stroking the heated skin beneath his silk shirt. 'I call you up and place you in the damnedest position—then drive around here in a rage, thinking *I'm* the wounded party because you send me off with a flea in my ear. I don't know how you put up with me.'

Because I love you, she said silently. Because I want so desperately for you to love me, too!

She moved to bury her face in his warm throat, drowning on a wave of desperate emotion. Her lips grazed his skin, eyes closing so she could absorb the pleasure in being close to him. Max trembled, and his arms tightened around her, his lips moved urgently to seek out hers, and they kissed—a long, clinging kiss, that spoke of desperation on both sides.

They were both a little breathless when they broke apart. Max looked down at her pale face, and spent a long time searching the unhappiness in her lavender-blue eyes. Sometimes—sometimes he could show such beautiful passion that she could almost convince herself that he cared for her more than he liked to admit.

It was this thought that made her reach up to place another gentle kiss on his mouth, and her smile came quite naturally as she combed the fingertips of one hand through his silky hair. Something strange passed over his expression. He caught the trailing hand and pressed a warm kiss to her palm, then their eyes locked in silent but obscure communication. Then he was turning her within his arm and leading her back to her bedroom, while Clea leaned weakly against him—self-pityingly, almost.

He sat her down on the bed and came down on his haunches, his ministrations indulgent as he helped her off with her robe and slipped her into bed, pulling the covers over her.

'Poor Clea,' he murmured, a hand stroking the side of her face. 'I don't remember these—women's problems —ever affecting you like this before.'

Her expression turned wary, instant defence stiffening her body. 'Damned hormones!' she mocked, smiling up at him as he leaned over her.

'Mmm.' His eyes twinkled their appreciation of her tease. 'Damned hormones.' He was squatting by her bed, one long, slender hand lost in her hair, the other covering both of hers. 'Shall we give tomorrow night a miss—hmm?' he suggested gently.

She pulled her hands from beneath his, understanding him exactly. 'Yes,' she said dully. 'We'll give it a miss.'

Clea supposed that she had asked for that. She had used the only excuse she could think of for her odd behaviour and, in doing so, she had ruined her last weekend with him. It shouldn't hurt that Max didn't want to see her just because he couldn't . . . but it did.

'How did your business dinner go awry?' She quickly changed the subject before the pain began to show. Max only wanted her for her body. She'd known that all along, so why should it hurt to hear him confirm it? Her chin came up proudly. Let it always be said of her that she bowed out graciously!

Max was straightening up, his expression suddenly dark, as though the memory of his wasted evening put a bad taste in his mouth. 'They—they didn't seem to know what they wanted,' he replied stiffly. Then his smile was back— to mask the other expression. 'You look like a child lying there,' he mocked. 'A rather forlorn, if charming, child.' He bent to give her a brief kiss. 'Sleep the weekend away if you want to. Maybe we both could do with a couple of quiet days,' he added with a touch of wryness. 'I'm expected home for a few days next week—can't turn up at my mother's looking half done to death! She'll nag me all the time I'm there if I do.' He was teasing her, urging her to look less the lost waif and more the self-contained Clea he had moulded her into.

'What about the theatre-tickets?' she reminded him.

He shrugged, moving away towards the door. 'I'll be sure to find someone who can use them.' He dismissed them as unimportant. 'Sleep well, Clea. Goodnight.'

Then he had gone, closing the bedroom door quietly behind him after one of his brief but brilliant farewell smiles, and Clea was left alone to listen to his closing the door of her flat with a finality he didn't know was there.

Monday morning found Max in a board meeting when the telephone rang on Clea's desk and a wispy voice asked to speak to him.

'I'm afraid Mr Latham is in a meeting and can't be disturbed,' Clea coolly informed the caller. 'Can I take a message, or get him to call you back?'

A breathy sigh. 'If you could just tell him it's Dianne,' the voice said. 'Then I think he would spare me a moment now.'

Clea frowned; she couldn't recall a Dianne from anywhere. 'I could buzz through and ask him, but he won't like it . . . ' Some strange instinct made her treat the caller with wary respect.

Another breathy sigh, that played on Clea's nerve-ends. 'Oh . . . ' sighed the voice. 'Perhaps it isn't *that* important . . . ' Then the woman giggled at something that eluded Clea. 'He *can* be rather forceful, can't he? And he *did* tell me not to call him at the office . . . but I . . . I didn't

know . . . Saturday night, when I saw him, that . . . '
Clea's stomach knotted, while the breathy Dianne trailed
into silence. 'You see, we should be having dinner again
tonight, but I can't make it . . . ' Clea sat like a statue, the
air around her suddenly too thick to inhale. 'I'm a fashion
model, you see, and I've been called urgently to Paris . . . '

Among the cries of shock that exploded in her head,
Clea registered the other girl's hesitation as an uncertainty
of her role in Max's life, and, even as she fielded the
numbing shock of finding out that there was a 'Dianne' on
the scene, she could sympathise with her. Uncertainty was
a way of life where Max was concerned.

'Will he be *really* cross at me for calling him, do you
think?'

Incensed, I would say, Clea thought bitterly. Max didn't
like ugly scenes, and Dianne's call was liable to cause a
humdinger of one if he found out about it. 'I tell you
what . . . ' She had to swallow to make herself heard
clearly, for the whole of her system seemed to have gone
into self-destruct. 'Why don't you call his apartment—and
leave a message with his housekeeper? He'll receive it the
moment he gets home, then, and you won't need to worry
about him becoming angry at you calling here.'

'Oh—what a good idea!' The breathiness was beginning
to grate. 'He really doesn't like his girlfriends disturbing
him at work, does he? I can tell by your voice.'

Clea recited Max's home telephone number, uncaring
that he would be furious at her giving it out so carelessly.

'You've been very understanding—thank you,' said the
breathless Dianne.

Oh, I'm full of understanding! scorned Clea as she
replaced the receiver. Little did the breathless Dianne
know that the last thing she wanted to do was pass a
message on to Max like that one!

Damn him! Damn, damn, damn him!

She'd known, just *known* it was coming to an end. Even without the baby to complicate things. She'd sensed it in him—seen the signs. But did he have to do it this way—find himself a replacement before he let her go?

Oh—Max!

He had come to her on Friday because the lovely Dianne hadn't come up with the goods. Heat rose in a prickly wave from her stomach to her head, and Clea made a lurching grab for her handbag and ran.

She made it to the Ladies just in time. With the toilet door locked behind her, she knelt weakly against the bowl and retched on the small amount of food she'd managed to keep down that morning. Limp and sickly hot, she stayed where she was for a while, breathing carefully when she wanted to gulp for air, and waited for her racing pulses to settle down. She felt like crying, but refused to allow herself the luxury. Max was seeing another woman, and that did more than hurt, it crushed her. She leaned her brow against the cool cleanness of the tiled wall, feeling the heat slowly diminish. If she got through the rest of today, it would be a miracle.

It was a while before she felt fit enough to leave the toilet cubicle. Mandy was leaning against one of the washbasins, her arms folded across her front, her pretty face concerned. Clea came to an abrupt halt, disconcerted to find her *malaise* had been witnessed.

'That was some performance,' Mandy drawled, her soft brown eyes searching Clea's pale face. 'I heard you, when I came in . . . You look awful, Clea. Shall I get Max to take you home?'

'No! No,' Clea repeated more calmly. 'I'm fine—really. I ate something last night that has been upsetting my stomach ever since.' The lying was definitely easier, she thought heavily, too easy for someone who usually prided herself on her honesty. 'I'm only glad that it's decided to come up at last. Maybe my stomach will settle down now.'

Mandy looked sceptical, to say the least, but forbore to say any more, lingering to watch Clea as she splashed water on her face then began letting down her hair, as though the severely confined knot was an unbearable irritation. She gave the glistening mass a shake, then started reapplying her make-up.

Mandy was madly in love with a big, tanned muscle-builder. He stood six foot three in his bare feet and was nearly as broad. She was older than Clea by five years, she was petite and pretty—and very wise. Clea wasn't sure if Mandy knew of her affair with their boss, but she suspected that she did.

'Is Joe in the meeting?' asked Clea. Mandy was Joe's secretary—and Clea's replacement if ever she was away. She flicked a comb through her hair, studying herself dispassionately in the mirror. She looked a wreck! Little Orphan Annie, she taunted herself, no one to love her and no one to love. She watched the bitter tilt that changed the shape of her generous mouth, sighing at it as she began covering the ravages of her recent nausea with a thin layer of foundation.

'Yes.' Mandy wasn't fooled by Clea's diversionary tactics, but she was prepared to go along with them for now. 'They should be finishing soon. I thought you'd be taking the minutes?'

Clea shook her head, her attention on her reflection. 'I've had to plough through the Stanwell contract. Max got Geoff Bradley's secretary to take the minutes—thank God! I detest those board meetings.'

'So do I,' Mandy agreed with verve. She was still levelling her shrewd gaze on Clea. 'Some more blusher,' she quietly advised. 'Under the cheekbones. Clea, why don't you stop seeing him?'

Clea went very still, her blue gaze flicking guardedly, to

look at Mandy through the mirror, her blusher brush poised half-way to her face. 'I—I don't know what you're talking about,' she prevaricated on an unsteady laugh.

'Yes, you do,' the other girl quietly insisted. 'Max is no good for you. You're too sensitive—too conformative in your ways to cope with his brand of living.'

Clea applied the blusher, then collected up her make-up utensils, her face suddenly very grave. 'Who told you?' she asked huskily. 'Joe?'

Mandy sighed heavily. 'You know Joe wouldn't say a thing to anyone. He's Mr Confidentiality himself. No, I saw the signs,' she revealed gently. 'Although you and Max have covered yourselves very well,' she hastened to add when Clea looked appalled. 'Take my advice and get out from under it,' Mandy appealed earnestly. 'He'll consume you if you don't.

Clea smiled at that, a tight little smile that gave a lot away. 'I'll think about it,' she clipped, then stood back to view the results of her labours in the mirror. 'Will I pass muster, do you think?'

Shut up and go away, her tone said, and Mandy's smile was lop-sided as she levered herself from the wash-basin and made for the door. 'You'll do,' she assured, then added on a dry note as she left the Ladies, 'Enough for him not to notice, anyway.'

And that said it all, thought Clea bitterly. It said it all.

It wasn't until after lunch that she had an opportunity to sneak in to see Joe. Max had kept her piled under with work all morning and Clea had been grateful for it—being busy meant she couldn't find time to brood. There was no use denying that the phone call from his latest conquest had knocked her for six. It had changed her whole outlook on what she was going to do about her future, and if there had been any weakening inside her to confess all to Max and let him share some of the burden—whether he'd be

angry or not—then the idea had flown out of the window.
She didn't even want to look at him, never mind hold a
personal conversation with him.

'How much of what I say to you here are you honour
bound to pass on to Max?' she asked Joe without
preamble.

He was sitting behind his desk, looking cool and
elegant in a dark grey suit and a crisp white shirt.
He was perhaps only about two years older than Max,
and very attractive. But in character, Joe was nothing
like Max. He was very much married, and content within
it.

His attention sharpened at the question, grey eyes
narrowing on her pale face as he tried to work out why
Clea felt the need to ask it.

'Only in as much as what you say will affect the
company itself,' he said levelly. 'I can be as confidential as
any doctor—until what you say crosses the line between
personal problems and company policy. Why?' he asked
quietly. 'What's the matter, Clea?'

Clea sighed, and dropped down in the chair Mandy
usually used. 'I want to give notice to leave,' she informed
him heavily.

Joe's fair brows rose. 'Without telling Max?'

Clea closed her eyes, nodding and swallowing at the
same time. Her hair fell around her as a black backcloth to
her incredible beauty. It wasn't just the perfect balance of
her features that made her stand out as something very
special, there was something almost sybaritic about her;
her eyes reflected a cool serenity, but couldn't quite mask
the innate sensuality of her nature, her mouth was too
generous—too pleasurably inviting for a man to believe
the impression of inner reserve she liked to portray. Those
long, thick black lashes did a lot to hide the real Clea right
now, and her mouth was being held in tight control, her

skin paler than it usually was. The black tailored suit she was wearing seemed symbolic, somehow. She was tall and slim, but the feminine curves were all there in abundance; full high breasts and a narrow waist, hips which curved deliciously, a stomach which was flat and firm. Clea had legs that any model would envy. But that cloud of blue-black hair, combined with an ivory smooth complexion and the biggest pair of pansy eyes ever seen, made Clea look, in every way, an exotic creature.

'Joe . . . ' She said his name on a husky sigh that stirred even his very married loins, and he smiled inwardly at himself for it. 'Will you let me work just a week's notice—and not tell Max that I'm leaving?' Her eyes anxiously appealed. His were narrowed and assessing.

He lifted an elbow on to the arm of his chair, his fingers playing absently with his clean jaw. When she had come in here, asking him if she could speak to him, he'd been alerted to something serious. But this? He shook his blond head thoughtfully.

'I think you'd better explain *why* you want such a quick release from your contract before I comment. And why you don't want Max told. He'll be furious—and you know it.'

Her full mouth widened into a semblance of a bitter smile. 'I should think that he'll be relieved,' she drawled, then tossed her head defiantly; sometimes her Latin blood showed through startlingly. 'It's over, Joe,' she told him heavily. 'Max and I are in the final throes of a staling relationship.'

Joe revealed surprise, then disbelief. 'Then why the cloak-and-dagger routine? Surely, if both you and Max are of the same mind, then there's no reason for you to leave the company behind his back.'

Clea shrugged her slender shoulders. 'We haven't actually discussed any of this. I just know it's time to get out . . . and I prefer to do it this way. It—it will be less embarrassing for both of us like this.'

Joe studied her narrowly for a long moment, while Clea trembled a little under his gaze. Then he got up, striding over to the coffee machine bubbling away in the corner of the room. He came back with two cups and placed one in front of Clea. The aroma made her stomach object, and she had to swallow on a lump of nausea. Joe watched her from his new position, half seated on the corner of the desk near to her.

'Are you pregnant, Clea?' he asked gently.

Clever Joe. Ever shrewd and perceptive Joe! With a muffled sob, as she stumbled from her seat, moving unsteadily over to the window behind his desk and staring blindly out, hugging herself as though cold.

Joe said nothing. Clea had just given him his answer with her reaction. She knew that as well as he did. He felt at a loss to know what to say. He felt furious with Max. But, above all, he felt sorry for Clea.

'Mandy mentioned about your—sickness earlier,' he explained on a shrug. 'I put two and two together . . . Have you told him?'

'No.' She hugged herself tighter.

'Don't you think you should?'

The waist-length mane of hair shook adamantly. 'He—he doesn't love me, Joe.' And it was all there, the pain, the misery, the fear and the heartache.

Joe's mouth thinned. 'He's very fond of you, Clea,' he said gruffly. 'I know he is.'

'No.' She refused to believe him. She looked so lonely, and young—painfully young, he thought.

'He'll think he has to marry me if he finds out,' she murmured, her voice so hoarse that Joe found difficulty in catching the words. 'And I can't let that happen. He'd hate me for it, I know he would.'

'You love him, don't you?'

'Yes.' She trembled, seeming to shake in a spasm that began at her shoulders and travelled down to her toes. Joe looked down at his feet. He was hating this. Clea was so proud, too proud to be reduced to this. He didn't want to witness it.

'You must tell him,' he stated grimly. 'He has a right to know.'

'Yes, I know,' she admitted wearily, still gazing out of the window. 'But he'll be angry—and rightfully so. It was my fault.' She waved an empty hand. 'I have this stupid mental block where taking medication is concerned. It was my fault, and I'll shoulder the responsibility on my own . . . I'll tell him,' she stated thickly, 'once I know what I'm going to do, once I have myself in hand again.'

'What about your parents?' Joe changed tack, he could see he wasn't going to get her to change her mind. 'They'll help you, surely?'

She turned at that, a wan smile on her too pale face. 'I'm certain they would—if I let them. But they've got themselves the most wonderful little love-nest going, and I can't intrude on that—not when they're only just getting used to being married.'

Joe knew her parents socially. He had been a friend of James's for years. It had been quite a joke at the time—when James had taken her and Amy to meet all his friends, and Clea found herself face to face with her personnel manager. 'They're so wrapped up in each other—it would be a crime for me to do anything to spoil it for them.'

Joe nodded solemnly in agreement. 'Then—what?'

Clea took in a deep breath and walked back to the desk, taking up a similar pose to Joe on the other corner. 'I'm not suicidal,' she said with an attempt at lightness. 'I'm not going to have an abortion. I have my flat, and I can

still work for a while yet, so I thought I would ring around
the secretarial agencies . . . '

'I may be able to help you there,' Joe cut in briskly.
'A colleague of mine is looking for a long-term temp,
who's used to computer jargon, to step in while his own
secretary visits her family in Canada. He runs a successful
software distributors; he might be grateful to you for
filling in. His secretary wants to make the visit a long
one—months, I believe—but she won't go unless she's
certain of her job on her return. She's an unmarried
mother, you see . . . ' His voice tailed off when he realised
what he had said, looking uncomfortable.

Clea touched his arm to tell him it didn't matter. And,
oddly enough, that aspect of her predicament didn't
bother her much. It was the practical side of it all that
concerned her. That, and losing Max.

'If you like, I could have a word with Brad,' Joe went
on. 'I think she intends going until September. How will
that fit in with . . .?'

'Fine—just fine,' she assured him. 'When does she want
to go?'

'Next month, if they could find a reliable temp. He
needs reliablity, you see. There's only him, his secretary
and a fleet of salesmen.'

'If I'll suit him, it would be a weight off my mind,' Clea
remarked, then added grimly, 'A-about telling Max, Joe?'

'I don't like it, Clea,' he told her bluntly. 'I don't much
like any of it. But we'll do things your way.'

Clea let out a sigh of relief. 'It will be easier this way,'
she assured him. 'I hate uncomfortable goodbyes. Max
will thank us in the end for doing it this way.'

Joe took to his feet, moving away from her with a
restlessness that spoke of a subdued anger. 'I'm not so sure
you're right about that. I simply can't believe that Max is
ready to let you go!' He sighed heavily and turned to face

her. 'I wish you would change your mind and tell him before you take such a huge leap into the unknown—he might surprise you. He . . . '

'He already has someone else.' She cut in on him with a quiet dignity that roused Joe's temper. 'So you see, I can't use—this, to hang on to him. He would never forgive me, and I couldn't live with myself for doing it.'

'Damn the bloody fool!' Joe exploded, his lean body stiffening with a need to hit out at someone—Max, preferably. 'He must be blind if he can't see just what he's passing up. You're too good for him, Clea—much, much too good!'

'Thank you for that.' She went to place a kiss on his angry cheek. 'I needed it.'

'Clea!'

'No.' She shook her head sadly. 'You must know I'm right, Joe. Let's just leave it now.'

CHAPTER FOUR

IT WAS late, and Clea and Max were up to their eyes in paperwork, trying to put things in order before he went away to Devonshire to visit his mother for what was left of the week. They worked in companiable silence, speaking only when it was necessary to the task in hand.

He had discarded his jacket and waistcoat during the day, his tie had followed soon after, and now he stood behind his desk with his white shirt-sleeves rolled back and his top button loosened, sifting through a sheaf of papers, while Clea sat in his chair, working on a set of papers scattered over his desk. It had turned dusk outside, and the lights in the office were on. Max had snapped the vertical blinds closed earlier in the afternoon, in order to block out a bright March sunshine. Now the room seemed cut off somehow; the building was almost empty, for everyone else had gone home long ago.

'Have you got the price list for the new keyboards there?' Clea threw the question over her shoulder without bothering to look up from what she was doing. 'I'll need to take some copies of it if you want the Buying Department to work from it while you're away.'

Like Max, Clea had removed her suit jacket; she had also tied her hair back at her nape with a piece of red waxed string to stop it clinging to her face while she worked.

Her enquiry drew Max's gaze to her, a reply ready on his lips, but his movements stilled when he caught the soft, ivory-smooth line from temple to jaw, left exposed by her tied hair. It was warm in the centrally heated office and her cheeks were delicately flushed. There was something distinctly vulnerable about her today, and the impression held him immobile while he absorbed the odd, twisting impact it had on his heart. Her eye lashes were long and black, curling luxuriously away from those wide-spaced purple eyes. Her nose was small and straight, her mouth pouting slightly as she concentrated, a rich, naturally red mouth designed for delicious kissing. She stood up unexpectedly, stretching across the desk for something, and Max felt his breath catch as he took in the sensual, curving shape of her, from slender shoulders to rounded hips.

Max felt the aching pull of her attraction reach right down to his loins, and the overflow of paperwork was forgotton while he allowed himself to experience the heated pleasure of just looking at her. She was wearing a white lacy bra beneath the blouse, and he could see the scalloped line where the lace finished and creamy flesh began. She sat down again, unaware of the way he followed her every move, taking pleasure in the sheer luxury of being this close to her. Clea never failed to ignite his senses—whether meant or unintentional. She was an instinctive sensualist—rarely, if ever, aware of her power over the male sex, yet always managing to achieve that air of deep sexuality that heats a man's blood.

The papers he was holding dropped on to the desk beside her elbow and, with sudden need to touch her, he placed his hands on her shoulders, moulding the rounded bones in his palms, feeling her instant stiffening reaction, watching the way she stopped what she was doing and lifted her head to stare directly ahead. She felt wonderful to touch. He hadn't realised how much he had missed her until his sensitive fingertips made contact with her smooth throat. She quivered when he ran his hands down her arms, then bent to place his lips where his fingers had just caressed, his hands moved to trap her in the chair by gripping the desk edge either side of her.

'You smell and taste delicious,' he murmured against the pulse beating madly at her throat.

Clea closed her eyes, trying to fight the wave of desire he awoke in her with just the simplest of touches. She wondered bitterly if Dianne the model smelled delicious, too.

What was the use? she thought on a long sigh. Max was touching her, here on prohibited territory, and she was no match against the rush of delight the realisation gave her. Her head tipped back to lean against his taut stomach, and Max moved his hands again, sliding them back along her arms until he found the open rever of her blouse, then slipping inside, to replace those lacy bra-cups with his warm and infinitely familiar hands.

His mouth was busy tasting her, the tip of his tongue licking at the warm flush of her cheek, running gently over her flickering lashes. His lips brushed a line down her nose until they found her mouth, nibbling and chewing with a hunger so real he shook with it, instigating an answering hunger within her that had her turning her head enough to join him in the slow, moist, passionate kiss. She lifted a hand to lay it against the side of his face.

'It's been a long time,' he whispered.

A long time. Did that mean he hadn't yet made it with the model? Clea thrust the thought away. She didn't want to think of Max with anyone else. She wanted to delude herself that he wanted only her.

On a wave of desperation she deepened the kiss, taking him by surprise by the violence with which she responded, and he shuddered as her tongue slipped into his mouth to stroke those sensitive spots she knew would drive him wild. Her blouse fell open for his urgent fingers, her breasts spilling out from the bra, now released, to expose her upper body to his heated gaze.

'Beautiful Clea,' he breathed shakily. 'What is it about you that bewitches me so?'

Clea turned, rotating in the office chair until she was facing him, their mouths never once breaking contact. Then she was on her feet and leaning against him, her arms going around his neck to pull him closer, as her body took fire in his arms with a need born of unfed love which made her fling all common sense to the wind.

Max trembled in recognition of what was happening. Sometimes—very rarely—Clea would respond like this, suddenly becoming a wild and hungry wanton, intent on a devastating seduction, and he felt that mood leap to life inside her now. The way she clung to him told him; she was kissing him almost tauntingly, her body moving against his in a manner meant to provoke him, until they were both breathless and gasping, eager to remove all the barriers preventing their heated flesh from touching.

His fingers were trembling as he released her from her skirt and helped it slither down her thighs, her blouse and bra already discarded.

'Undress me,' he commanded unsteadily, his hands sliding down to press her lower body fiercely against his own, eyes closing on a pained groan as red-hot needles of desire shot through him, making him press her even closer. 'Clea,' he cried, unable to let go of her so he could remove the unbearable barrier of his own clothes. 'Help me, Clea. I need... *need* you!'

Her arms clung to his neck, fingers buried in the dark silkiness of his hair. She leaned back a little in his embrace, and looked languidly at him. 'Lock the door,' she whispered, her breath sweet torment against his heated face.

He looked dazed with desire, his cheeks flushed, 'Yes, yes.' He put her from him shakily and went quickly to turn the key in the office door.

When he spun back to face her, Clea had moved away
from the desk and stood by the deep alcove, beside one of
the deep leather chesterfields. Her pose was provocative,
almost illicit in its blatant invitation, and he felt the flush
of desire run helter-skelter over his skin. Clothes felt too
confining, as if they would constrict his breathing, and he
began dragging them impatiently from his body, his hot
gaze glued to her pale, voluptuously curved flesh. She was
looking at him in the same hungry way, her kiss-swollen
lips parted, lovely eyes dark with need.

Max's skin shone with a healthy tan, his chest broad and
deep, liberally covered with dark, curling hair. Hips,
lean and taut, legs, long and muscular, his body rippled as
he began walking slowly towards her, prolonging the sweet
agony while those liquid eyes beckoned to him and her
tongue-tip came out to lick a moist circle around her full
mouth.

It stopped him momentarily, his breath leaving his lungs
on an unsteady hiss. He was so aroused that he could feel
every pulse-point inside him throbbing urgently, then
begin hammering when she offered him a seductive smile
and lifted her arms to remove the piece of string from her
hair. The action lifted her breasts, setting the creamy flesh
quivering, the dark brown centres with their long, hard
tips seeming to reach out to him in invitation for his
hungry kisses. Her hair tumbled free, and she shook the
black mane so it fell in a glistening tumble of raven silk
around her shoulders and arms, tendrils of the fine stuff
caressing those wonderful breasts.

'You're a witch,' he accused hoarsely, moving swiftly
now to reach her in two strides of his long legs. He took
her shoulders and dragged her against him. Clea laughed
up at him, head tilted back in open provocation, lips
parted, waiting for the burn of his kiss. He glared down at

her, face muscles rigid, a flush streaking his taut cheeks. 'A gypsy enchantress.'

Those sensual lips pouted, eyes taunting him, and she murmured something in Italian to him, her voice pitched low and huskily erotic.

'Clea,' he choked, 'have you any idea what that does to me?'

He had no idea what she was saying to him. That was part of the pleasure she gained from switching to her father's native tongue. Max couldn't speak or understand Italian, so he had no idea how she told him all those things she dared not say to him in English.

Clea wound her arms around his neck, leaning the lower part of her body against his and smiling at the pulsing tension she encountered. 'Love me, Max,' she invited softly, in English. 'Love me.'

It was too much for him, and he groaned, having to close his eyes for a moment while the shuddering reaction rippled pleasurably through him.

Then they were kissing urgently, and their movements were rough—aggressive, almost. He lifted her and carried her to the space between the two settees, lying her down on the soft piled carpet and coming down beside her.

He homed instantly on to her breasts, laughing in throaty triumph as she arched beneath him when his mouth sucked on one hard, throbbing tip. His hands trailed her silken body, their light touch sensitised to the exquisite shape and feel of her.

Their loving became a strange battle to see who could torment the other the most, Clea finding ways to please him that sometimes overwhelmed him into total stillness. She was different tonight, he noted within the vague recesses of his mind, almost desperate to taste and feel every inch of him. As though . . .

'Oh—no!' He snatched her away from him, pulling her back along his body when her moist caresses threatened to pitch him over the edge. 'What are you trying to do to me?' he groaned, but didn't give her an opportunity to reply before he was pulling her beneath him.

She welcomed him on a soft cry, her silky limbs cocooning his thrusting body against hers, her eyes closed, hair in wild disarray around her passionate face. Max held her to him, his arms trapping her body against his, his face lost in her throat when, on a final groan, he gave himself up to the pleasure that was the woman beneath him. The end came in a disintegration of anything earthbound, and it was on wave after wave of hot liquid sensation that he felt himself being drained of what seemed, to his dazed mind, to be his life's essence.

It was a long while before Max found the energy to lift his heavy weight from her and move to lie at her side. What they had just shared had astounded him, moved him beyond imagination, and he opened his eyes to look at her in wonder. Clea's lids were lowered, her beautiful face revealed a similar wonder to his own. He reached up to gently remove some clinging strands of hair from her damp cheek, his expression unusually exposed. She opened her eyes, taking him by surprise and catching, before he could mask it, the look that had stripped him of all the shutters he usually wore.

'I'm coming home with you tonight,' he told her huskily.

Clea shook her head. 'No, not tonight.' She refused him quite gently. Or ever again, she added sadly to herself. I've just said goodbye to you, Max, in the most beautiful way I knew how. 'You have a lot of work to get through before you can leave here tonight.' She smiled, to take the sting out of her refusal, reaching up to tenderly comb her fingers through his tumbled hair. 'Think of your mother!' she teased lightly. 'And how she'll nag if you turn up looking haggard to death.'

He didn't join in the joke. His mouth tightened. 'I'm coming home with you,' he repeated, with a touch of defiance.

'No.' She sat up, arching her back to ease the ache lying on the hard floor had caused. Her head was thrown back, and the long flow of waving blue-black hair brushed the carpet. Max watched her, his mouth pulled into a thin line. Clea let out a contented sigh, then got to her feet, her movements all natural grace, no self-consciousness.

She turned slowly to face him, her head tilted to one side, and smiled a gentle, loving smile at him. He was frowning, puzzlement creasing his brow, aware with a certainty now that something had altered in their relationship. She even *looked* different, though he couldn't put his finger on exactly why.

'You've scattered your clothes again,' she rebuked in a teasing vein.

Max grimaced, but didn't smile. He was in no mood to be coaxed into good humour. Clea was on the run from him. It had hit him as she had turned and smiled at him like that. Clea was backing off from their relationship.

He came to his feet in one lithe movement and brushed tersely past her, ignoring her completely as he pulled on his clothes. After a few minutes spent watching him, she did the same, saying nothing. The silence was a new one, it was cluttered with the unspoken word, with angry questions and evasive replies.

Dressed again, Clea contemplated him for a moment. He was back at his desk, sifting through the mounds of paperwork, once more the cool businessman.

'If it's all right with you,' she said levelly, 'I'll leave now.'

His remote glance touched her only briefly. 'It seems I have no say in the matter,' he drawled, in such a cold voice it made her flinch inside. He lifted a long hand and waved it towards the door. 'Go—go, by all means, go.'

It was over. Clea lingered by the door, trembling slightly as she let her eyes greedily drink him in for the last time.

I'm having your baby.

'Changed your mind?' The sound of his voice, softened yet taunting, jerked her out of her sad absorption, and she blinked, smiling slightly, at herself, not at Max.

'No . . . No, I haven't changed my mind,' she said quietly. 'Goodnight. Max.'

If he made any reply, then Clea didn't hear it. Yes, she thought painfully. It was definitely over.

Clea stepped outside the railway station and looked around for the distinctive steel-grey head of her mother's new husband, James Laverne.

She had called Amy earlier in the week to invite herself down for the weekend. Joe had let her leave work early on her final day, a leaving that had been sadly quiet, since only Joe and Mandy knew of her going. Her new job started a week on the following Monday, which meant she had the whole of next week to get used to all the changes affecting her life. Max was in the past. She had to learn to accept that now, even if the ache of acknowledgement was sometimes unbearable.

Amy had been delighted by Clea's intention to stay a few days. Her light laughter had come down the telephone line to fill Clea with a surge of homesickness for the sight of her mother's dear face.

'Oh—that's wonderful, darling!' Amy had exclaimed. 'It will give me an opportunity to tell you my marvellous news—well, two pieces of news, really,' she amended drily. 'But they're both marvellous.'

And I have some less marvellous news for you too, Mother, Clea had thought rather bitterly. She didn't relish the announcement at all, and could only hope that her news wouldn't cast whatever Amy had to tell her into the shade.

'Clea!'

More female heads than just hers turned to follow the long strides of the tall, elegant figure of her new stepfather. Clea grinned at him, dropping her weekend case on the ground so she could put hands on hips in a provocative stance as he approached her, eyeing him up and down in the guise of an appreciative connoisseur.

'How my mother was lucky enough to catch you, James Laverne, I'll never know!'

She found herself wrapped in a bearhug of an embrace before James came back with a reply. 'You know as well as I do who was the lucky one, miss, so you can stop the teasing right now!' James was smiling lazily, his sharp blue gaze searching her pale face, taking in in an instant the changes in her since they had last met.

They walked together to where James had parked his car, James carrying her case and stowing it in the back of the luxurious Rolls before climbing in behind the wheel and heading them towards home.

'You look peaky,' he observed bluntly once he'd negotiated the car into the steady flow of commuter traffic. His glance swept briefly but thoroughly over her then returned to the road ahead. 'You know I would have collected you from work and saved you a train journey. Why do you look peaky?' he pressed on sternly. 'Amy will go spare when she sees you.'

'I look "peaky", as you so nicely put it, because I've just recovered from a rather inconvenient tummy bug.' She had no intention of blurting out the truth to James. Confession time would come later, when Amy was there, too. 'And I couldn't ask you to pick me up, because I had no idea what time I would be leaving the office . . . And

Mother always finds something about my appearance to worry over—whether I'm in blooming health or lying at death's door!' She shrugged expressively. 'It must all be part of being a mother, I suppose, looking for trouble when none is there . . . ' Clea threw James a teasing glance. 'I bet she mothers you to death!

James grinned, his lean, handsome face softening on thoughts of his new wife. 'And the rest,' he admitted ruefully. Then he shook his head with some more ruefulness. 'I still find it hard to believe that she actually gave in and married me. She was so *offended* when I first told her how much I wanted her!' That steely head shook again, his expression saying a lot about how James treasured memories of his courtship with Amy. Clea felt an automatic lessening in the tension that had gripped her for days now. Amy and James were like two star-crossed adolescent lovers, the way they behaved. It seemed unbelievable when you considered that, for the reputedly hard-bitten, successful stockbroker he was, when James had fallen for her mother, he'd lost seven tenths of his cynicism and *all* of his forty-six-year-old-bachelor ways.

'The mistake you made was in the terminology,' Clea thought it fair to point out. 'It's the word "want" that offends, not the actual wanting.'

James nodded, looking suddenly thoughtful. He glanced shrewdly at her, his blue eyes too all-seeing. 'I have a feeling that was spoken from some experience?'

She shrugged the question in his tone away, turning her face to the side window so he couldn't probe any deeper beneath her fragile defences. 'How's the Stock Exchange?'

There was only the slightest pause while James absorbed the fact that she was deliberately changing the subject, then he launched into a fascinating tale about the ups and downs of the unpredictable Exchange, and his talk continued all the way to the lovely mansion house he shared with her mother.

Amy was waiting at the door when they drew to a stop, her loving embrace encompassing Clea the moment her feet stepped on to the driveway. Clea stood a good five inches over her blonde-haired, petite mother, but their hugs were equal, both physically and spiritually.

Tension slid from her shoulders like a heavy mantle lifted away. Could it only be a week since that fateful visit to the doctor? It felt longer—much, much longer.

CHAPTER FIVE

CLEA sat in front of her dressing-table mirror, staring at her freshly made-up face, and wondered if she had managed to cover up the ravages of the last week enough to fool her mother. Amy was sharp, and had already sent Clea some frowning looks before she had managed to escape to her bedroom, on the pretext that she was in desperate need of a long soak in a warm bath. The latter had been true to a certain extent, and she had indeed indulged herself in the soak, but only as a way of delaying the return back downstairs. Now her time had run out, and dinner would be ready in a few minutes.

Her eyes clouded, apprehension and the ever-present heartache mingling to form a constriction in her throat. The next few hours were, perhaps, going to be more difficult than her next meeting with Max. And she didn't relish *that* much—or doubt that it would take place once Max had found out about her defection from his employ. He was going to want to know why, and she was going to have to tell him.

One thing at a time, Clea, she advised her reflection, realising how once again she had let her mind wander to Max. Max! The perpetual ache contracted into a sharp pain she was beginning to associate with his image.

Sighing unhappily, she applied just a shade more blusher to her cheeks before getting up to check the snug fit of her red mohair wool dress. Long-sleeved and cowl-necked, it moulded her slender shape to her firm hips before flowing out to swirl gracefully about her knees. Red suited her. Max liked her in red, he said it enhanced the incendiary quality in her she liked to think was well hidden . . . Stop it!

She spun away from the reflection. If she carried on like this she would be in no fit state to go downstairs; her nerves were already jangling with dread. At least her slim shape showed no signs of what was happening inside her body—except, maybe, in the dark smudges beneath her eyes that were not entirely due to worry, but also a constant awareness of an unsettled tummy.

With a determined pushing up of her chin, Clea made for the door and went slowly downstairs, convincing herself that she was ready to confess all.

But in the end things didn't work out quite like that, because her mother revealed her news before Clea could conjure up the right words to broach her own problem.

They had reached the coffee stage after a superb meal, unspoiled by guilty confessions. The conversation had been pleasant and relaxed, with only the three of them at the table to enjoy the intimacy of soft lighting and beautifully prepared food. Clea had just been dragging her courage together in readiness to break her news, when Amy excused herself from the table and disappeared out of the room for a moment, coming back with a long envelope that looked faintly ominous, which she placed in front of her daughter. Then she stopped Clea from looking inside by placing a dainty hand over hers.

'The first of my surprises,' she announced smilingly. 'You will be twenty-one years old in a month's time.'

Clea's eyes widened. So she would be! The magic number! People officially 'came of age' at eighteen these days, yet the old tradition still lingered in most people's hearts as the 'real' age to receive the proverbial key of the door.

'This——' Amy tapped the envelope '—is by way of an early birthday present . . . Open it,' she allowed at last.

'And then I'll explain properly.'

Baffled, Clea picked up the envelope, slowly drew out the high quality paper and opened it out with decidedly shaky fingers. A long and complex-looking official document lay on the table before her, and Clea's puzzlement increased as she stared at it, unable at present to make head or tail of the elegantly scripted words printed on it.

She lifted a bemused gaze to her stepfather for insight. 'What is it?' she appealed breathlessly. 'I don't understand . . .'

James was smiling at her, his blue eyes gentle, and as if by second nature he reached out to clasp one of Amy's hands. 'It's an endowment policy,' he enlightened gently. 'Taken out in your name, at the time of your birth, by your father.'

Clea stared blankly at him for the moment it took for those words to sink in, then shifted her gaze to the document—and felt a sudden flush of love run through her.

'When he—your father—died,' James went on quietly, 'your mother continued the payments. It matures on your twenty-first birthday.'

'F-for me?' she repeated huskily. 'Daddy took this out for *me?*'

'You know what he was like, darling,' her mother put in warmly. 'So old-fashioned and—and *Italian!* It was meant, I think, as a dowry, outmoded in this day and age, I know, but it was what he intended and I was determined to carry through his wishes.'

Clea saw, through her own blur of tears, how Amy's eyes had glazed with soft but sad memories. 'Oh—Mummy!' she choked, clutching that tiny hand that held on to her own. It was too much—too much! And coming at a time when she felt she had let her beautiful parents down!

'The reason I'm telling you about it,' Amy went on more briskly, 'is because I need your signature to release the money the endowment has accrued.' Then, when Clea remained too full up to say anything, Amy squeezed her hand and said huskily, 'This has nothing to do with James and I . . . It is your father's gift, given to you with all his love.'

'How will I ever thank him?' Clea sobbed, crying quietly and without restraint.

'In your heart, darling,' Amy answered gently. 'He'll hear your thanks there.'

James simply listened and looked on, faintly envious of the deceased man who could still command this much love from his family. After allowing the two women to weep for a while, he took in a deep breath, then broke into the emotional storm with a delicate clearing of his throat. 'You haven't even asked how much,' he pointed out mockingly.

'I don't care,' she replied on a sniff, then broke into a husky giggle. 'How much?' she then asked immediately, her eyes twinkling at James.

He named a figure that shocked her into stillness. She heard little of James's knowledgeable explanation on how some endowment policies accrued money by wise investing throughout the years; all Clea could think of was that her father had done this with her future in mind—because he loved her, and because he wanted the best for his daughter. She had sullied that love with her foolishness; it cast a scar deep into her heart to realise it. She had dishonoured her father and the clean morals he had instilled in her through his own high moral beliefs. She didn't deserve this, and worse—even as she was thinking it—she was aware of feelings of relief because of what the money would mean to her future.

Amy turned bright eyes to her husband—misreading the expression skittering across her daughter's pale face. 'Oh, James!' she sighed. 'How can Paolo be dead, when he sits here looking at me through my daughter's eyes?'

It said a lot for James's confidence in Amy's love for him that he could accept such an emotional outburst, and Clea's own estimation of her new stepfather doubled as she saw his gaze soften with sympathy.

'Now, Mum,' she rebuked teasingly, to break the grip emotion had on the room. 'You and I both know just whose eyes I inherited.'

'Colour, shape, size.' Amy nodded in agreement. 'But the expressions you use are all your father's.'

'I think we'd better retire to the other room,' James inserted with a rueful tilt to his mouth. 'Before all this emotion threatens ruin to my Queen Anne table!'

They walked out together, James flanked either side by a beautiful woman, both as opposite as the poles, yet unbreakably tied by the sheer strength of natal love.

Clea went very quiet once she was seated in the luxuriousness of an easy chair of champagne velvet. Her brow was creased into a brooding frown as, with each passing minute, it became more and more difficult to say what she knew she had to say. James was fussing around Amy, seeing her seated on the settee before going to pour them all drinks, handing them out before going to sit beside his wife, again reaching for her hand, as though physical contact was imperative to his well being.

Clea felt a stab of envy rip through her. Amy was so lucky! She seemed to have everything her daughter yearned for—the love of a good man and . . .

'What was your other piece of news?' she asked suddenly, again delaying the moment when she would have to confess. 'You did say *two* bits of news, didn't you?' she prompted, when she was surprised by the look of sheepish embarrassment that reddened both faces opposite.

Amy and James looked at each other and their glances lingered, silent messages passing from one to the other while Clea sat watching it happen with a vague feeling of uneasiness. It was her mother who turned to face her, looking as uncomfortable as Clea felt.

'I—I'm not sure how you're going to take this, darling.' She began with the warning so as prepare her daughter. Clea straightened slightly in her seat. 'I—that is, we—James and I——' poor Amy blundered, her cheeks going redder and redder. 'That is—well . . . We're going to have a baby!' she announced on a rush. 'I don't think it is at all the done thing at my age. But—well, it's happened, and really . . .'

Once started, it seemed Amy couldn't stop her self-conscious tongue, and she ran on while Clea sat, stunned, trying desperately to come to terms with what her mother was telling her.

She felt like giving in to hysterical laughter. There was a distinct buzzing going on inside her head, and all she could do was stare across the space separating them, shocked into complete immobility. She knew her face had drained of all colour, because she felt it happen—just as she knew if she didn't get rid of the glass from her hand she was likely to snap its delicate stem.

She dragged her eyes away from her mother, and with a studied care set the glass down beside her, all the time aware that James was watching her with narrowed eyes. The sky was falling in! she found herself thinking with tragic fancy.

'Will you mind, Clea?' she heard her mother ask anxiously, and made a concerted effort to pull herself together.

'Of course I don't mind!' she exclaimed, managing to sound convincing because it was the truth. She thought it was the best thing that ever could have happened to them. 'I think it's marvellous news! Nothing—nothing could be more complete than for you and James to have a baby of your own!'

'I'm thirty-eight years old!' said Amy balefully. 'To—to be quite frank, I feel a fool!'

Clea blinked, glancing furtively at James who was still watching her with a narrow intensity that hinted at anger. What was he thinking, she wondered, to make him look at her like that? Amy's free hand was fluttering nervously, and Clea returned her attention to her mother, realising that whatever was bothering James would have to wait, because she could see her mother was looking pretty frantic.

'Don't you—want the baby?' she asked bemusedly. They had so much to give a child, she couldn't believe it was possible that they weren't over the moon about it.

'Of course we want it!' James answered sharply, and the anger she'd seen in his eyes showed in his voice now, though he tried to contain it when he spoke again. 'Your mother is feeling a trifle—vulnerable just now, that's all.'

Clea struggled to pull her ragged thoughts together, her stunned mind grappling with the irony of it all. 'When is it due?'

'October...'

October!

She saw, through a frantic haze, her mother smile shyly. 'October the fifth or thereabouts—you know how it is.'

Oh, she knew how it was all right! She was going to get a new brother or sister, and become a mother herself, all in a space of a few days!

'Well——' She made herself get up and squat in front

of Amy and James, her limbs stiff and trembling in shocked reaction, taking a hand from each and squeezing them urgently, her smile brilliant enough to blind. 'I think it's wonderful!' she said. 'Accept my congratulations.'

Damn yourself, Clea! she inwardly berated herself. And damn Max Latham, too!

By the time Clea escaped to privacy of her own room that night, she felt emotionally shattered. It had become obvious from the moment her mother had told her about the coming baby that Clea could not spoil their pleasure by blithely saying, 'Snap!' And, as her shock dimmed and she'd begun taking note of Amy's nervous anxiety about her condition, she had to determinedly thrust all her own problems aside to set about convincing her mother and James that having a baby now would be wonderful for them.

James was quiet, and coolly withdrawn. And Clea knew he had sensed something in her attitude, seen, maybe, her initial reaction and was angrily puzzled by it. James adored Amy, but he was still vulnerable enough in his feelings to be highly sensitive to others' opinions of his new role—especially Clea's opinion. For, if James valued anyone's blessing, then it was his stepdaughter's because he was very much aware of how close mother and daughter were.

What a mess! She had come here for the express purpose of baring her conscience, so that she could then get herself in hand before having to face Max. Now all she seemed to have done was add to her own troubles, and her head ached with the weight of them.

It was ridiculous, she sighed, leaning back in her bed to stare at the darkened ceiling. Like living on a balance scale, she likened with bitter humour. One minute up, the next down. Surely things couldn't become more complicated than this? Soap operas, eat your hearts out! she scorned.

She was becoming a nervous wreck. Quiet, level-headed Clea Maddon was learning that the Fates could rock anyone's self-possession—except Max's, maybe. Clea couldn't think of a single thing that could manage to shake him!

I'm having a baby! God, what was she going to do? And how many times had she asked herself that question recently?

It was just gone eight o'clock when Clea crept silently down the stairs, dressed in jeans and a warm V-necked jumper over a brushed cotton blouse. It was unusual for Amy and James to be up at this time on a Saturday, and she hoped to be able to make herself a pot of very weak tea before having to face them. She was, therefore, brought up short on entering the kitchen, to find James already there, seated at the table with the morning newspapers scattered about him.

He glanced up and smiled at her. 'Tea's fresh in the pot,' he invited. 'Your mother is staying in bed a while longer—the dreaded morning sickness, you know.'

Oh, Clea knew! She had personal experience of it.

'I've got into the habit of taking her a tray up with the statutory slice of dry toast and pot of weak tea,' he admitted, with a touch of rueful mockery meant for himself. It must feel rather strange to James to find himself in this position at his age, but Clea had an idea that he was thoroughly enjoying his new role of prospective father.

'Does it work?' she enquired as she pulled out a chair next to him and sat down.

His grin was wry. 'It makes the—er—giving up a whole lot easier, I think,' he quipped, then shrugged. 'Amy believes it helps and, in the end, that's all that matters.'

Clea studied him over the rim of her cup. He really was

pleased with himself; it showed in every word he spoke—no matter how flippant he was being. 'I suspect it's the pampering she's getting from you that does more good.' She wished there was someone who would pamper her, love her as much as James loved Amy . . . Her gaze dropped to her cup; James was forgotten for the moment while she drifted off into a miserable world of her own.

James watched her thoughtfully, his grey gaze flickering over each strained feature on her pale face.

'Come for a walk with me,' he invited suddenly, getting up from the table and tapping her hand to gain her attention. 'Come on,' he insisted when she looked reluctant. 'It's cold but fresh outside. It may do us both good.'

Clea complied, seeing no way out of it without offending him. It was certainly cold outside, and she huddled into her leather blouson, the collar turned up around her ears, hair caught in a high ponytail so that the heavy tresses swung as she walked in easy silence for the length of the beautifully laid-out garden. James indicated to a garden seat set beneath an early-blooming blossom tree, and they sat down.

'It's nice here,' Clea sighed, glancing dully around her. 'I like the house. It has a sturdy, dependable look about it.' It was built in red brick, and had attractive, domed bay windows with criss-cross leaded glass.

She felt James humph on a grimace. 'Add "like me", and I think I'll have to slap you,' he muttered, then let out a sigh of his own. 'Sometimes I feel my age.'

'Forty-six isn't old, James,' Clea dismissed wearily. Her gaze was trained on the house, her body slouched in the seat, hands lost in her jacket pockets. 'I wonder, sometimes,' she went on in the same tone, 'if my visits here are solely for the benefit of convincing you two love-doves that you are not over the hill!'

James was watching her, his expression grave as he followed the drawn line from high cheekbone to turned-down mouth. She was tall and beautifully formed, her long legs, stretched out before her in tight jeans, only emphasised her sleek shape. 'You came here this weekend to find solace, I think,' he remarked quietly.

Clea threw him a guarded glance. 'Like—flying back to the nest when "the little black rain cloud" settles over one's head?' she mocked grimly, then slid her gaze back to the house. 'Not bad, James,' she congratulated a trifle bitterly. 'No wonder you speculate in the City so successfully.'

'But instead of finding your much-needed solace,' he went on, refusing the warning she'd just issued in her tone. 'You find yourself further bogged down with—little surprises!'

'The pun is in the word "little", I presume.' Despite herself, Clea had to smile.

'Does it bother you?' he enquired. 'To be getting a brother or sister at your age?'

'No,' she answered abruptly, and honestly, proving it by looking directly into his eyes.

James accepted this with a grimace. 'Then it must be your love-life that's bothering you,' he assumed levelly.

'Define "it" for me, will you?'

He smiled at that. ' "The little black rain cloud," ' he mocked. Then, more seriously, 'Something is certainly troubling you, Clea. I thought, last night, when I noted your reaction, that it was our news that had hurt . . . And I have to admit, that made me angry. I thought that you maybe saw your mother's condition as being somehow unfaithful to your father's memory.'

'No!' she denied hotly. 'Never! James, how *could* you think such a thing? How could you think I'd be so petty?'

A grim smile twisted his mouth. 'She's mine,' he stated

flatly. It was he who was avoiding Clea's affronted look now. 'I acknowledge that your father has a place in her heart that I can never trespass on. But she's mine now, Clea,' he repeated harshly. 'And I . . .' the smile twisted again, and he dipped his head to stare at his shoes '. . . I'm very touchy about hanging on to every bit of space left.'

'Oh, James . . .' Clea's heart went out to him, and she touched a gentle hand to his arm in understanding. 'Mummy loved Daddy,' she said gently. 'I can vouch for that. But when you came along that same unstinting love was transferred to you! Forgive me when I claim to know her better than you do as yet. My father was a fine man, and we both loved him dearly—and missed him terribly when he died. But what happened to Mummy when you came into her life will always be, to me, the finest thing that ever could have happened to her . . .' She looked fondly on his hard, handsome, yet vulnerable, face, and swallowed the lump forming in her throat. 'And James—I *know* Mummy loves you now more deeply than she ever did my father.' His head snapped around at that declaration, utter surprise forcing him to search her face for sincerity. He found it. 'That wasn't easy for me to say,' she admitted solemnly. 'But it's the truth, none the less. Her love for my father was of the young and innocent and rose-tinted kind. She was never disillusioned by it because my father adored her enough to ensure the glasses stayed in place. Her feelings for you go far deeper—believe me.' She smiled wanly. 'What she and my father felt for each other made the chances of any other man taking his place a virtual impossibility, yet you did, James. And to me that shows that Mummy's feelings must go deep—for how else could you compete with a ghost? She loves you, James.' Clea patted his arm firmly. 'And you can be sure that Daddy has simply swapped places with you in her heart—or why else would she have married you? She could have lived the rest of her life on just the memories of that first love, but she didn't.'

James stared at her, a flush colouring his lean face. He shook his head wryly, and covered his embarrassment with a mocking smile. 'You sometimes completely throw me, Clea,' he murmured, then lapsed into a brooding silence while Clea returned her attention to the house—and her own heavy thoughts.

'Thank you,' he said after a while.

She shrugged indifferently. 'For what? It was only the truth, after all.'

'And who has come along to eat his way into Clea's heart to make her so perceptive of others' feelings?' he probed softly, noting the slight stiffening in her body. 'It wouldn't be the infamous Max Latham, would it?'

Clea's hand left his arm to be thrust back into her pocket, her generous mouth tightening a little. 'How much do you know about Max and me?' she asked tightly, not looking at him.

James sighed and shook his head. 'Only that you see a lot of each other, and that the—er—relationship seems—close.'

'By that,' she muttered 'I suppose you assume we are lovers!'

'Well, if it isn't Latham,' James persisted, 'it has to be some man who's managed to turn you into a woman since I first met you. You were an innocent then, Clea,' he stated gently. 'I haven't lived this long without learning to recognise innocence when I see it.'

Clea made a sound of impatience. 'Does my mother know?' She didn't bother denying it. James was too clever by far, and he was going to find out the rest of it soon enough, anyway.

James let out a husky bark, startling several small brown sparrows into flight. They fluttered away, twittering in protest, and Clea watched them absently. 'Amy?' he laughed. 'You're her little girl, still,' he told her drily. He let out another bark of amusement as a thought came into his mind. 'When she informed me that she had a young daughter at home, I imagined a sweet little pigtailed angel formed in her mother's piquant image. Imagine my feelings, Clea, when I saw you!'

Clea couldn't help but join in the humour of the situation. It must have come as a ridiculous surprise to him, for Amy did have a way of describing Clea as her 'little girl'. And her appearance had always been a source of amazement to others when they saw her with her mother. She and her father used to delight in the notoriety, because Amy was always so baffled by people's surprise.

'I remember thinking, "My God! I've fallen in love with the wrong Maddon." '

'James!' Clea protested, shocked.

He threw her a speaking glance. 'I'm not blind, Clea,' he informed her a trifle witheringly. 'You are a very beautiful and sexy lady—not——' he continued when she gasped at his choice of words '—the child your mother sees. And, even being fathoms deep in love with Amy as I am, it doesn't stop me from appreciating a lovely woman when I see one. Max Latham isn't blind, either,' he added carefully.

Her gaze wondered frontwards again. 'It was wonderful while it lasted.' She used mockery to hide behind, then dropped it because she was tired of hiding, tired of the lies and prevarication. 'It's all over now,' she said quietly.

'And you needed a bolt-hole where you could hide to lick your wounds?'

'Something like that.'

James looked at her pale profile with tender sympathy. 'He's—he's well respected in the City,' he pushed on carefully. 'He got the Stanwell contract, didn't he? It put his share price up a tidy bit.'

Clea eyed him curiously. 'Got some yourself?' she asked.

'A few, when the price was lower,' he drawled, and waved a slender, dismissive hand. 'But I won't sell. Latham is still on the way up—not down.'

'Yes.' She didn't need James to tell her that. Max knew where he was going, and the path had no twists in it: a direct ascent, with no one in tow.

'What did he do to you, Clea?'

'I don't work for him any more,' she used as a reply, her tone dull and so retracted that James had to gather himself to probe further.

'He—dispensed with your services?'

'No,' she grated. 'I left of my own accord.' Everything they said held another meaning. Clea shifted irritably on the bench, her face turned almost fully away from him now.

'You were the exception to a very strict rule, so I heard.' James was aware that he was teetering very close to the edge. He could actually feel the tension in her. 'And one that has lasted a hell of a lot longer than his norm.'

She turned bitterly on him. 'Has Joe been gossiping?' She started to get up, but James stayed her with a hand on her arm, forcing her to sit down again, and holding her there.

'Joe is no gossip, and you know it. I'm in the business of having my ear to the ground,' he reminded her gently. 'And it really is very interesting what one eavesdrops on in the process.'

Clea snapped her lips tight shut, and sat in mutinous silence while James waited, holding her arm, though she wasn't pulling away from him. He could feel her trembling, and felt a hot sting of anger rip through him, aimed at the handsome Max Latham.

'Why don't you just give in and tell me about it?' he persisted. 'You know I'm not going to give up until you do.'

'And why don't you just mind your own business?' Clea blazed, but the angry blue eyes she turned on him were full of a terrible pain.

James held his ground. 'Amy is my business,' he stated firmly. 'And what affects you will, in the end, affect her.' He paused, sighing impatiently at her mutinous expression.

'It may help, you know, to tell someone... I'm a good listener, Clea. Offload it on to me,' he urged on. 'You'll feel a lot better for...'

'With no editing?' she sneered. 'All the sordid bits as well as the——'

'Stop it!' James cut in harshly. 'There's no need to get insulting!'

'I'm pregnant!' she cried, then let loose a broken sob. 'I'm pregnant . . .'

James muttered something beneath his breath, his eyes revealed a level of shocked anger Clea would never have thought him capable of; then he was masking it and reaching over to grasp both her hands where they ripped at each other on her lap.

'Latham's?'

'Yes,' she hissed, shivering with reaction.

'And he—he won't marry you?'

Her quivering mouth twisted on a smile that made his heart contract. 'He doesn't know,' she told him bleakly.

'But—Clea . . .'

She threw back her head, her eyes too big in her pale face, and stared at the frosty blue sky peeping through the branches above them. 'He doesn't love me, for Heaven's sake!'

She slumped forwards, tugging her hands free so that

she could cover her face as the floodgates at last opened and she broke down altogether.

James sighed heavily. 'But you love him, I presume.'

'Of course I love him!' she croaked, lifting a hand from her face to wave it towards the house. 'You don't get brought up by someone like Mummy without some of those high morals of hers rubbing off on you! Of course I damned well love him!' she cried wildly. 'I just—just wish I didn't, that's all.'

'Hell!' muttered James. 'Did we put a great hulking spanner in the works when we let go with our bit of news!' He leaned his elbows on his knees, staring at his feet in grim contemplation, then he glanced up at Clea. She was back in control of herself again, but those huge eyes were filled with aching tears. 'When is it due?'

She glanced at him, then away. 'October.'

James gasped, then looked stunned—then, to her dismay, he began to shake—shake with laughter while Clea looked on in fury.

'It isn't funny!' she snapped.

'It's damned well hilarious,' argued James. 'October the—what?'

'Eleventh—James, will you stop laughing at me?' she demanded when he set off again. 'I can't tell my mother now! She'll—she'll miscarry with the shock!'

That sobered him up. And they both sank into dark reflection on the bench at the bottom of the garden.

'No, she won't.' James spoke at last. 'She's not as frail as you and I like to think her to be. She can take it.'

'I disagree,' protested Amy's daughter. 'It will break her heart!'

'It will if you don't tell her,' James pointed out. 'Amy loves you, and she'll understand. And she has me . . . We'll go and tell her now,' he decided firmly, grabbing Clea's hand and forcing her to get up. 'You and I together will go and tell her, and Amy will cope, because we'll put it in such a way as to give her no choice.'

'Like how, for instance?' Clea muttered derisively. 'Like, "Now you've got to see the funny side of this, Mummy, but—surprise, surprise . . .!" '

'Sounds fine to me, put like that,' said a determined James, pulling his reluctant stepdaughter behind him back to the house.

'But James . . .!' She tried appealing to him, but it was no use. They entered the kitchen to find Amy already there, looking the picture of maternal contentment.

She turned to smile at them both. 'What have you two found so interesting to talk about out there? I thought you were taking root, you've been gone so long.'

James went to his wife, kissing her soft cheek tenderly before taking her hand and sitting her down at the table. He gestured to Clea to sit down, too, then placed himself opposite them both and reached across the table to take both Amy's hands.

'It seems, darling,' he said gently, 'that, in our eagerness to tell Clea our news, we quite stole her thunder, because she has her own very special piece of news to tell us.'

Amy looked wide-eyed and curiously at James, then turned that same regard on to her uncomfortable daughter.

'But what could that be, Clea?' she puzzled, then let out a gasp of delight. 'Oh—you're not going to marry that nice Mr Latham, are you, darling?'

'Amy, dear.' James patiently reclaimed his wife's attention. 'You misunderstand a little. You see, Clea isn't going to marry Max Latham, but she's going to do the next best thing when he's the man she loves.' Clea listened, white-faced and sobbing inside. 'She's going to have his baby.'

CHAPTER SIX

BY THE time James drove Clea back to her flat on Monday evening, she was feeling more at peace with herself.

'I know it's all been said already—several times,' James murmured into the companiable silence surrounding them inside the luxurious Rolls. 'But you are more than welcome to come to live with us.'

'Yes, I know. And I'm terribly grateful for the offer,' she replied sincerely. 'But I won't take you up on it.'

If the truth were to be known, she felt tempted. Her mother and James had spent the weekend veritably cocooning her in a security blanket of love and understanding. But she would not allow them to do more. It wouldn't be fair—to either them or herself, in the end.

'Because of me?' James queried quietly. 'Would you have given in to your mother's urges for you to stay if your father had been alive to add weight to her arguments?'

'No, not for the reasons you're implying,' she answered gravely. 'There are a lot of reasons why I'm determined to "go it alone", as the saying goes. Not least, the very newness of your marriage, the fact that you are both—no matter how deeply in love—still learning to know each other. I wouldn't, and don't want to, intrude on what you have and deserve . . . I can't honestly say whether I would have moved back home if Daddy were still alive, but I think not. I'm used to being my own person now . . . living with Mummy again would be—restricting.'

'Stifling, I think you mean,' James corrected wryly, then flashed Clea a knowing grin. 'Oh—I'm not completely blind to Amy's faults, you know. She likes to wrap the ones she loves in cotton wool—she likes to wrap me up like that, but I don't mind, where you would suffocate, I think.'

'I love her dearly,' Clea felt constrained to say, because James was surprisingly correct in his view.

'But all the more so from a distance,' he added drily, and they both laughed, because neither meant any malice towards small, fragile Amy. 'And—Max?' James questioned carefully.

She shrugged. 'I'll tell him about the baby the first opportunity I get.' It had been a decision reached with her mother yesterday. 'Though I feel guilty for thinking it, I have to say that Daddy's gift has eased my mind of some of its worst worries.'

'Now you know I would have helped you there, Clea!' James admonished sharply. He was wealthy, after all; money was not one of James Laverne's problems.

'You and Max both,' she agreed a little bitterly. 'Do you think I'm not aware of that? And if I do find I need any help of that kind, I promise to come and tell you instantly. But it isn't in me to sponge off others' generosity, James. Call it false pride, if you want.' She shrugged those delicate shoulders again. 'I suppose it must be pride, because I know for sure I can't take a thing from Max, and he has more right to this than either you or my father.'

'Well, you won't have to *beg* from anyone now,' James said mildly, his voice holding a certain satisfaction in its tone. 'By the time the policy matures I'll have worked out some scheme to make the money work for you. You should, with careful investing, be able to live off the income from it. I'll see to that.'

'And my flat will be fine for bringing up a child,' Clea added, as though they were playing a game of 'count your blessings'. 'I was brought up there myself, so I should know.' She fell into sombre meditation for a while, staring out of the window while James drove them smoothly into London. 'It won't be the financial side of my plight that can cause Max any concern,' she added quietly, as though really voicing the thought out loud rather than to her stepfather. 'I should be able to convince him now that he need feel no obligation towards me and the baby.'

'And at the same time prove to him that you weren't out to trap him,' James concluded shrewdly.

She didn't reply, but her heart twisted painfully. James was right, she knew that *that* would be one of the accusations Max would throw at her. But it wouldn't be fair or true. Conceiving their child had been an accident. She just hadn't got the hang of taking those damned pills on a regular basis! She had missed more than one.

Naïvité was no excuse for what she had allowed to happen. But she admitted to a shameful naïvete about taking those precious little pills. Now, on looking back on the last five months, Clea found herself wondering in amazement that it hadn't happened earlier!

Her mind slipped back to that first time, when protection had never entered either mind. They had become too lost in each other to think of anything beyond the sensual banquet they were sharing. It had been later, when heartbeats had steadied, that Max had mentioned protection, and asked if she wanted him to take care of it, or whether she would like to. And she'd thought how much easier it must be to just take one small pill each morning rather than worry about the other options open to them. So she'd said that she would take care of it, and the subject had never arisen again. But Clea now knew herself to be guilty of not going into the rights and wrongs of pill-taking. She had just presumed that if she missed one that she could take two the day after to make up for it. When that ran into taking three on occasion, she didn't think to question the reliability of such inconsistency.

Oh, Max! The quivering ache, that seemed to have become a natural reaction to thinking of him, came to torment her again. Along with it, the ever-loving image of that devastating smile he could switch on when he felt like it, his eyes bright with wicked humour, his dark face a hard and ruthless background to such sensual charm. She could see him as he looked in the morning—a morning when he didn't have to rush off to work, so he would instead stretch himself out on her sofa while she prepared breakfast, his black hair ruffled, face unshaven, eyes sleepy. He would wear only the trousers of his suit, and lie there with his long bare feet sticking over the edge of her sofa, wide chest rising and falling to the rhythm of his breathing while he scrutinised the Sunday papers. Lazy as the sloth, tanned arms rippling as he turned newspaper sheets, short dark hair curling down from his chest to the concaved tautness of his stomach and further, burrowing beneath the waistband of his zipped but unbuttoned trousers.

At those times, he could have been anyone's husband relaxing at home. So utterly unaware of himself that Clea used to have to bite on her lip to stop a wistful sign from escaping in case he might hear it. Max was beautiful in any guise—unkempt or impeccably groomed. He was a man who wore his worth in the power of his personality rather than the clothes he dressed it in.

The flat was quiet and felt faintly unwelcoming. And, even though the central heating was pumping away to keep the temperature at a steady seventy-five degrees, Clea shivered with a chill that came from within.

She was glad James hadn't delayed his departure. He had seen her inside, deposited her suitcase in her bedroom, then left, wanting to get back to Amy. And perhaps he'd sensed that she wanted to be alone, had seen in the clouded look in her eyes that she needed time to compose herself, come to terms with what lay ahead of her.

She was tempted to call Joe and find out how Max had taken her desertion when he'd arrived in work that morning, but she knew it would be the wrong thing to do. Joe had done enough. It was time to stand alone and take whatever was coming to her square in the face

Max.

By nine o'clock, she was beginning to relax. She had gone around the flat switching on lamps and plumping up cushions. The smell of fresh coffee filled the air, and she had unpacked her case, showered and changed her clothes for a comfortable suit of fine hand-knit wool in a rich electric-blue colour. The skirt was lined, and swished against her silk-clad thighs as she moved, the cowl-necked, batwing top felt soft and warm against her skin.

She was about to sit down in the lounge with a cup of coffee when the doorbell went. She felt herself go cold, the small hairs on the back of her neck rising in instinctive warning, and she had to force her body to move towards the door, because every muscle had suddenly gone heavy with dread.

With a nervous finger-combing of her long, loose hair, she reached for the door latch, not bothering with the safety chain. She didn't peep around the aperture but opened the door wide, her gaze already levelled on the man who had come to see her.

It was Max.

He was certainly dressed for the part, Clea mused grimly as she stood to one side to allow him room to enter her flat. Black trousers that hugged his lean hips. A black leather windbreaker over a black silk shirt and black V-necked sweater. The Angel of Death! she thought with bitter fancy.

He made directly for the lounge, barely offering her a

glance, other than the one grim expression as he faced her at the door. She closed the door and followed him slowly to find him standing in the centre of the room, outwardly relaxed—and a stranger.

'When did you get home?'

An air of grim resolve circled him, making his presence oppressively felt in the room, and Clea shivered a little. 'About three quarters of an hour ago.'

She ran clammy palms down her skirt, hovering uncertainly by the lounge door for a moment before coming further into the room. He lifted those heavy lids to watch her, and it was then that she saw the melancholy, the complete lack of understanding, and she had to look away, move somewhere—anywhere, so long as she didn't have to stand still and face him.

Prickly heat began to run up from her feet—another symptom of her pregnancy, this inability to control her own body temperature under stress. Desperation made her sit down abruptly while he remained standing, looming over her. Silent, waiting, as was his manner when he felt unfairly treated. He wasn't going to make this easy for her. Max wanted answers, and, after all, they both knew the questions.

She made a play of straightening her skirt, her body stiff with tension, sitting on the edge of the seat like some self-conscious teenager. Her hands were shaking, she noticed with agitation, so she clasped them together on her lap, then forced her face to lift so that she was looking up at him.

'I—I've been away.' She began at the end, because the beginning was too impossible. 'Visiting my mother.'

Silence. He just continued to stand there, looking gravely at her, and Clea felt a sob of anguish rise to her throat. She swallowed it down. He looked about as approachable as a Highland bull! If he would only remove his jacket then she would feel a little easier. No, that wasn't true; the removal of his jacket would indicate a prolonged stay. She didn't want that at all.

'D-did you find *your* mother well?' Hedge all you like, Clea, she told herself wryly, when he continued to stand and stare grimly at her. He was going to ignore anything she said that didn't stick ruthlessly to his reason for being here.

She had never seen him so still before. Max was usually a livewire of restlessness. Even when relaxing, he fidgeted—couldn't keep still.

'OK, Max,' she sighed wearily, giving in under his silent pressure. 'But—but will you please sit down!' She waved him to a chair. 'It's intimidating having you stand over me like this.'

He continued to stand over her long enough to set her nerves screaming, then moved to do as she bade, taking the other easy chair, situated next to her own, folding up his long frame and crossing his legs in a haughty, waiting pose that made her shift uncomfortably.

She glanced furtively at him to find his hard gaze steady on her pale face. Her lids lowered, dark blue eyes unable to meet and hold blue.

She heaved in an unsteady breath. 'I'm sorry if it made you angry, my going behind your back to Joe . . .' Once again, she began nearer the end than the beginning; she couldn't seem to help herself. All that careful planning she had done with her mother seemed to have flown out of the door, on Max's arrival, to leave her floundering. 'B-but I thought that this way it would be—l-less embarrassing for both of us . . . I start my new job on Monday,' she added, for some reason known only to her frantic mind.

'He told me.' Max spoke at last, and Clea flinched at the softness of the sound. How much had Joe told him? She dared a swift glance at his face, but Max was revealing nothing.

Clea sent the pink tip of her tongue swiftly around her lips, and tried again. 'It—it was better this way. No bitterness, no fuss and tense atmospheres . . . You must see that I was right.'

'I don't *see* anything yet!' he pointed out. 'I'm still waiting for you to make it all clear to me.'

I'm having your baby. 'It's been an odd week, one way or another . . .' She laughed nervously at the stupid remark, and noticed absently that her hands were slowly mutilating one another. I feel very young suddenly, she thought. Quite unable to cope with the situation. Max was sitting next to her, only a foot away, his long legs drawn up and crossed at the knee, hands resting comfortably on the chair arms, dark head turned in her direction—and a face so hard it could be made of stone. Did he know how attractive he was? How infinitely crucial he was to her existence? Did he know that she loved him and that this was tearing her apart inside? She sensed that he did. But what was more important to Max were the 'whys'. He didn't like puzzles of any kind, that was what made him such a whiz on a computer; give him any intricate problem to solve and he would gnaw away at it until he'd solved it. And that was why he was here tonight, not because he was hurt by her defection, or because he was concerned for her. He just needed to know 'why', that was all.

The silence lengthened again, and stretched until it was singing shrilly in her ears. It must have got to Max, too, because he sighed suddenly, a long, heavy sound, then flicked a long-fingered hand as though affecting the throwing in of the towel.

'I presume,' he drawled, 'that this——' He was at a loss as to what to call the situation. She couldn't blame him, she had no name for it, either. 'This *surprise* waiting for me when I got into the office this morning, was by way of announcing an end to our association?'

At least he hadn't called it an 'affair'. Even Max, it seemed, had some scruples. 'Yes,' she murmured huskily. 'It couldn't go on any longer, Max. Not when . . .' *I'm having your baby.* 'When I—I realised . . .'

'Realised—what?' he prompted softly, when once again she dried up. And the quiet snap in his voice made her flinch a little so that she veered off course yet again.

'Joe was very good about it. He—he found me a job, with a friend of his. It seemed to work in very well. Then I went to visit my mother this weekend, and she dropped her bombshell on me, and everything began to get . . .'

'Clea——' Max cut in on her wearily, almost anxiously, but then she didn't know how she looked, couldn't see herself as he was seeing her at this moment, her lovely face contorted with unhappiness and stress. 'You're rushing on like a steam train, but I can't follow a single word. Let me say something,' he ventured drily, sitting up a little in his chair and leaning closer to her. He sounded more human now, more like the Max she knew, and when she dared a quick glance at him, she could see that he looked more approachable, his eyes warmer, his mouth not so tightly drawn. 'Look at me,' he insisted gently, and she turned her face up to him, eyes big in her pinched, pale face. 'For some reason known only to you,' he began quietly, 'you've decided to bring an end to our relationship.' Clea preferred that to 'association', it had a more intimate ring to it. 'I can't say that I'm surprised because, quite frankly, I'm not . . . I suspected something of the kind before I went away last week. But what I don't understand is why, and that is why I'm here tonight.'

Just as she'd supposed, Clea thought heavily. He watched her face, misread the abject misery there for fear, and sighed impatiently. 'I'm not going to throw things at you, or shout——' though he was near to doing that now '—I just want to understand, then I'll leave again... Does that make it easier for you to explain?'

No, it made it harder! Because it proved that she'd been right all along and he didn't care for her at all.

I'm having your baby!

'I own this flat, Max,' she informed him thickly. Her frantic mind was groping for the right words, the way to say that small remark that would make all of this sensible.

'I know you do,' he sighed. 'But . . .'

'And this weekend, while I was at my mother's . . .' she trudged on, ignoring his impatient interruption. 'And she dropped two surprises on my lap, one of which doesn't concern this now, but the other does . . .' She took in a deep breath and held on to it. 'I have my twenty-first birthday coming up next month . . .'

'Clea—you're losing me again!'

'Then let me finish!' she bit out, the tension in her pulling her delicate skin taut across her cheekbones. 'I have to explain this my own way! I have a birthday coming up,' she repeated heavily. 'And my mother gave me this—this endowment policy—taken out by my father when I was born. It matures on my birthday. It's for a lot of money. James said . . .'

'And who the hell is James?' Max bit out angrily. He looked as confused as Clea felt. His black brows drawn into a straight line, eyes flashing silver-blue fury. 'The man who's usurping me in your bed?' he enquired derisively. 'The man who . . .'

'James is my stepfather!' she enlightened witheringly.

'James Laverne,' she told him, her own expression as derisive as his now, as anger at him made her forget everything else but looking disgustedly into his face. 'I have mentioned him to you before but, as usual when I tell you anything personal, you haven't bothered to listen properly. James Laverne is a stockbroker—a very successful one. And he's going to invest the money, so I won't have to worry about an income for a long time. So . . .' She dragged in another deep breath. 'I have my flat, and no financial worries.'

'Which adds up to—Clea being of independent means, and therefore no longer in need of a well paid job with me.' He thought he'd solved it, and his mouth twisted unpleasantly, his sarcasm cutting into Clea so she had to struggle to maintain some composure.

'I left your employ *before* I knew about the money,' she pointed out cuttingly. It was all right for him to mock, but he didn't know what all this was leading up to. 'And,' she added tightly, 'I already have another job waiting for me.'

'So it's only poor Max who's being given the elbow!' he concluded, on a crack of dry humour.

Anger made her jump up from her chair to stand glaring at him. 'And could *poor Max* give a damn?' she sliced back bitterly. It was decaying into a slanging match as she had known it would.

'Not if scenes like these are to be the norm from now on, no,' he drawled. 'I don't think I do give a damn.'

'Good,' she said, fielding his contempt, with only a flicker of her lashes to reveal how his words had hurt her. Cold purpose pushed up her chin. 'Then knowing just how you really feel about me makes it a lot easier for me to say what I've been finding difficult to tell you.'

At last! his long-suffering expression said.

'I'm going to have a baby.'

There, it was out. She had actually said it, and relief

made her sag a little.

But Max didn't sag. Clea had to watch the mask of cold condescension slide away from him, watch those blue eyes narrow into angry slits, watch that lazy body pass through the stages of coiling up in reaction. His hands went stiff, then clenched into fists, his spine arching convulsively and his face rife with furious colour before paling to a stage beyond anger.

Real fear made her put out a shaky hand towards him in appeal. 'Let me explain . . .'

'You bitch!' he whispered, and Clea fell back a few steps as, on a low animal growl, Max launched himself out of the chair, hard hands snaking out to clutch at her quivering shoulders before she had a chance to move out of his way.

'It was an accident, Max——'

He wasn't listening, his fingers crushing the fine bones beneath them, eyes like silver points of violence between their frightening slits. 'I trusted you!' he bit out roughly, and shook her hard.

It was like looking on the face of a stranger; anger contorted his face, held his jaw clenched and his lips pulled back from glinting white teeth. She whimpered, jerking up her hands to clutch at his wrists, in an attempt to make him let go of her, but he only increased the pressure.

'I trusted you!' he repeated, his voice so thick that he was barely understandable. 'You were going to take care of it!' he grated in a rough, whining voice meant to mock her own assurances all those months ago. 'And all the time you were planning this!'

'No!'

'Yes! You bitch!' He shook her again, the whirl of blue-black hair a mad tumble around her paste-white face. 'I trusted you—I *trusted* you!'

Then another thread of his control snapped, and Clea

had to watch in horror as his arm went back, hand hovering above her while his blanched face told her what he meant to do.

'Don't——' she tremored. Fear sent her own arm up to protect her face, and she cowered in his grip. Then the heat began, surging with incredible swiftness up and along her body until it reached her ears where it roared, blocking out everything else.

Max, the arcing hand and his biting grip on her upper arm all became insignificant as she began trembling violently, quivering from head to toe. The pressure inside her head increased, balls of brightly coloured lights propelled themselves against the back of her eyes and exploded into a million excruciating fragments, and she whimpered again, a pathetically weak sound, just before she felt herself go heavy. Then there was nothing, absolutely nothing. Blackness assailed her, and thankfully gave her an escape route.

CHAPTER SEVEN

MAX watched in a kind of horrified fascination as Clea crumpled to the floor in a deep faint. The angry hold he'd had on her was insufficient to halt her fall, so that all he could manage to do was control it a little, numbly watching the way her arm, once released, fell heavily against her limp body.

The utter silence in the room buzzed in his ears; the actuality of what he had almost done still damning him, for his right arm was still raised in readiness to strike. The shock of it wiped his face clear of everything but appalled horror at himself.

He stared down at the inert heap of electric-blue wool and flailing black hair, swallowed tensely, then fell to his knees beside her, gently turning her over and away from the arm that still protected her face from his pending blow. Everything about her looked blue, her clothes, her hair—and even the frightening pallor of her skin.

'Clea——' he breathed hoarsely, shocked by his own actions, by the way he had caused this to happen. Then he was sucking in a deep breath of air and pulling himself together, scooping her limp frame into his arms and carrying her to the sofa. She was heavy in faint, boneless. He had never seen her looking so ill and vulnerable before. It gave him a harsh twinge of self-disgust to acknowledge that it was directly due to him that he was seeing her this way . . . Oh, God, Clea!

He began rubbing gently at her cold hands, but there seemed to be no circulation getting through; her skin was opaque in patches, the pressure of his fingers leaving indentations in the pale, lifeless skin.

'Clea——' he urged huskily, willing her to come around.

She did so slowly. A small nerve flickered at the corner of her mouth, then her eyelids fluttered and life seemed to seep back into her limbs, making her stir a little.

Max continued to rub at her hands, and it was upon them that she focused her confused gaze first. Then, as painful memory returned, she stiffened, pulling free of his grasp and lifting very wary eyes to his.

'I wouldn't have done it.' He rushed into denial, his voice rough and rattling. He looked as white as a sheet, shock holding his jaw rigid. 'It was reaction. I wouldn't have hit you.'

No? Max had lost complete control of himself for those few terrifying seconds. She had always considered his self-control formidable. Now she knew that wasn't true. And she had no wish to incite him to that point again, so she remained very still and said not a word, letting her lids slip downwards again while she tried to steady the shakiness still clamouring inside her . . . Max had almost hit her, and her shock to this was almost as debilitating as the fear that had enveloped her for those few pole-axing seconds.

He was watching her; she could feel his concerned gaze on her as she lay. To his eyes, she seemed to be still struggling with faintness, but really she just didn't know how to handle the situation any more and was using her faintness to hide behind. His breathing was the only sound in the quiet oppressiveness of the room, short and rasping, as though he, too, was labouring under shock.

He moved away after a while, going over to where she kept the brandy. Poor Max, she thought wearily. He hadn't known what was going to hit him when he'd arrived here tonight with his sombre face and cool words of understanding.

'Drink some of this.' He was back at her side, running an arm around the back of her shoulders to lift her a little.

Clea flinched. 'Don't touch me,' she whispered, dragging herself up to lean on the arm of the sofa and away from him, running trembling fingers through her hair. He held the brandy glass between clenched fingers; she noticed the tension in them, and felt a twinge of satisfaction that she had managed to throw him this much. But she took the glass from him, acknowledging the necessity of the harsh spirit.

The foul-tasting stuff burned her at the back of her throat as it slid down, and she grimaced, but at least she felt some warmth filter back into her and was able to pass the glass back to him with a steady hand.

He moved away again without a word, and Clea lay back against the sofa arm, feeling utterly drained. Her head was throbbing, and her heart was pumping out slow, heavy beats that sounded in her ears. It was inevitable, she supposed, as bitterness once again welled up inside her, that things should have come to this. It didn't help her to know that she'd handled the whole scene very badly. That her stupid emotions had all become knotted and in the way of a clear, calm and precise explanation. Stupid, unwanted things, like love and need and fear of the aloneness she was going to have to face, had all come to complicate everything for her. But what she struggled with now, in the heavy atmosphere of her lounge, was the hard and fast realisation that she'd been hoarding a secret hope that he would prove her completely wrong and react in a way that would make her heart sing.

Now she knew, and her thin smile was full of self-derision.

She pulled herself into a sitting position, sliding her feet to the floor and pushing her tumbled hair from her pale face. Max was slumped in the chair, his lean body hunched over his spread knees, eyes brooding on the glass of brandy dangling from long fine-boned fingers.

'It was an accident,' she muttered huskily into the silence. 'You were a fool, Max, to get involved with a naïve idiot like me.' Clea sighed as she leaned wearily back against the sofa, watching him dully. 'I took those pills in good heart. I was just too stupid—or badly informed—to know that I couldn't afford to miss taking them with the regularity I was doing. I don't want anything from you,' she told him clearly, so as to make that point plain, if nothing else. 'It was my error, and I'll take full responsibility for the consequences.'

'We'll get married,' he responded quietly, as though she hadn't spoken at all. 'As soon as I can arrange it, we'll get married.'

Clea made a sound of tired impatience. 'Have you listened to *anything* I've been saying tonight? You don't *need* to marry me!' she cried in weary exasperation. 'By several strokes of good luck, I'm in a position to have this baby without you having to give up your precious freedom. I don't want to marry you, Max,' she told him bluntly. 'You aren't my idea of good husband material.'

His head jerked up at that, and Clea saw how pale and haggard he looked. Good, she thought, at least that shows he isn't going to come through this completely unscarred. Then his lip curled, and he looked more like the cynical Max she knew well.

'Don't be stupid!' he clipped. 'This is no longer a matter between just you and me. We have the child to consider . . . We'll get married, and that's all there is to it. No child of mine is going to grow up in a one-parent situation. He'll have *my* name, and *my* support and protection—just as *you* will have, too.'

'And what about love, and trust, and fidelity?'

'Are you referring to me?' he enquired haughtily. 'You know, without my having to tell you, that I'm—fond of you.'

'Do I?'

He waved a dismissing hand at her, his expression restless and vaguely uncomfortable. 'And the other two you've always had from me. We'll make a success of it—for the child's sake, we'll . . .'

'I know about Dianne Stone.' Clea dropped in gently. James had supplied the full title to fit the model. She was a tall, sylph-like blonde, and very beautiful. Clea had seen a picture of her in a copy of her mother's *Vogue* magazine. She'd felt that beauty cut into her like a knife, because Dianne Stone had something that Clea only pretended to have: sophistication, a 'must' if you intended to have an affair with Max.

She watched, with detached interest, the guilty colour run up his face as he stared blank-eyed at her, and Clea allowed herself a bitter smile. Caught you in one move! she thought. Now get yourself out of it! She was momentarily shocked by her capacity to hate him as she did at this moment; hate was the one emotion she had never expected to feel towards Max.

He shot abruptly from the chair, thrusting his hands into his jacket pockets as he moved jerkily over to the window, reaching out to lift the curtain a little, so he could gaze broodingly out on the dark night. The quietness had a dull thump to it now. The kind you get when all other emotion has been well and truly done to death.

'How did you find out?' He didn't even attempt to deny it.

'She rang the office to speak to you,' Clea told him.

The muttered oath from the window area was self-explicit and unrepeatable. Clea pulled a wry face at his right to be angry. Max went to great pains to cover all contingencies—to keep his life running on that straight and tidy path he'd plotted for himself.

'I'm sorry that had to happen,' he said gruffly. His back was stiff, the hand gripping the curtain white-knuckled against the dark red velvet.

For some unaccountable reason, that gruff apology seemed to signal the end to her self-control. Clea felt the weak tears flood the back of her eyes, and dropped her face into her hands, crying quietly when she knew she should be exhibiting strength and presence of mind. It happened so unexpectedly that she found she hadn't sufficient resources to stem the flood once it started. She felt so cold and alone, hurt and very, very vulnerable. It was all so—so—*sordid*!

'God, Clea, don't cry!' Max was suddenly beside her, squatting by her chair and trying to pull her into his arms. She fought him off, refusing the comfort he was offering, refusing his pity. She wished she was alone now, to hurt in privacy. She wished he would just go!

But he wouldn't go. Max wasn't feeling comfortable enough yet to turn and walk away. His hands came up to cover hers, fingers curling around hers in an effort to force them away from her face, his touch achingly familiar, the slight tremor running through him an indication of the fraught state he was in.

He held her hands tightly, forcing her to look at him through sheer strength of will. 'It was never my intention to hurt you, Clea,' he murmured roughly. 'Dianne—Dianne was a mistake. Already in the past! She was nothing but a——' He pulled himself up short with a snapped closing of his taut mouth, whatever he'd been going to say severed before it made any sense to her. His gaze sought hers with anxious urgency. 'We can make this work for us!' he insisted. 'You can't go through this on your own—and I don't want you to. I want . . . I want to shoulder my share of the responsibility.'

He had been doing so well until then, she had even felt a slight weakening in her stubborn resolve—until then. Now, frantically, she shook the dark fall of hair. 'I *won't* marry a man who thinks I trapped him into it. I *won't* marry a man who was already looking about for someone else!'

'You're *wrong!*' he grated. 'I am—very fond of you. No! Don't turn away from me! I won't let you cut me out like this!'

Fond? God! Had he *no* idea how much that hurt? 'No!'

They became involved in a pathetic struggle, she trying desperately to free herself from his urgent grasp, he determined to make her stay still and listen. Their ragged breathing was the only sound in the fraught atmosphere of the room. And suddenly, it seemed that the tables had turned, and it was Max taking the defensive stand, and Clea the offensive—although neither seemed to be aware of it.

'*Fond* isn't enough!' she choked. 'I don't want you to be fond of me. I don't want you to "shoulder your responsibility"! I couldn't live with it, don't you see?' She appealed for understanding, violet eyes wide with misery and bright with looming tears. 'You would hate it!' Clea dragged in a shaky breath and tried to calm herself. 'You value your freedom more than anything else. You don't w-want to be m-married, tied down to one w-woman. You couldn't cope! Your whole foundation is built around your freedom of will.'

Max stared at her, stunned into speechlessness. He searched his mind for his defence, and found, with a shock, that he had none. Abruptly, he sat back on his heels, his hands leaving her to fall on to his spread thighs, dark head lowering in defeat.

'I'll make a drink.' Clea struggled out of the chair,

needing to get away from him before she gave in to the desire to take him in her arms and comfort him. For Max was suffering a little at her hands, and the gentle side to her nature was appalled by her own ruthlessness.

The kitchen was a relief after the tensions of the lounge, and Clea hovered there, delaying the moment when she would have to return to whatever awaited her in the other room, because she and Max had by no means finished.

This time it all had to be said, a conclusion reached—and accepted on both sides. And, before she faced him again, Clea knew she had to sort her swirling thoughts into some kind of comprehensible order.

Surely he must have some idea how she felt about him? But then, she reminded herself wearily, Max had never been interested in her, Clea, the person, not really. He saw only the shape of her body. His interest had been in the sensual woman who warmed his bed and delighted his senses, or the super-efficient woman who ran his office; but not Clea, the person, not *her*.

Max had never asked for her love. He had asked for nothing but the regular use of her body when he'd desired it. It wasn't his fault that her reasons for allowing him the liberty were widely different. She had accepted his terms five months ago, and he couldn't now be blamed for her own folly. But now he would accept her terms—and her chin came up proudly as she picked up the laden tray—because hers were the right ones to deal with an impossible situation.

He was hunched in the chair when she entered the lounge, elbows resting on spread knees, brooding again. Clea put the tray down and poured two mugs of coffee, passing him his in silence and receiving a silent nod of thanks in return.

'When did you find out?' he enquired once she was settled in the chair beside him.

'The Friday before you went away.'

He grimaced as some daylight dawned. 'No "friend" on a visit to London, then?'

'No, no friend.' By no stretch of the imagination could she call her doctor her friend. She took a sip of coffee. 'I had an appointment with my doctor; he confirmed my suspicions.'

'And you spent the rest of the day in a state of shock,' he presumed wryly as his mind flitted back to that awful day.

Clea nodded. 'While you had your *business dinner*——' she couldn't help the dig, it just came out '—I used my *quiet weekend*——' another dig, and Max winced '—to decide what I was going to do.' She took in a deep breath and let it out again, sounding weary as she continued. 'You were planning on being away from Tuesday, and it seemed an ideal opportunity for me to make the break without it causing too many—problems. Joe was very understanding . . . He guessed almost immediately what was wrong——' Damn him, she thought wryly. Max was thinking the same by the look on his face.

'He never gave a hint of it to me.' He confirmed her thoughts by accusing roughly. 'He just said you'd asked for an urgent release from your contract and that he saw no reason for not giving it you. I gave him plenty of reasons!' he added angrily. 'His actions were tantamount to being disloyal to me!'

'That's not strictly true, Max,' Clea argued quietly. 'Joe simply weighed up the situation and used his own experienced judgement. Your being informed any earlier would have caused friction—and made no actual difference to the final outcome.'

'Want to bet?' he challenged gratingly.

Clea smiled, but let that go. Max might believe he had the monopoly on character strength, but he didn't.

However, she wasn't going to argue the point with him just now.

'When is the baby due?'

She'd begun to think he would never ask. 'October,' she said, then let out a laugh that had nothing to do with amusement. 'Do you want to hear something quite bizarre?' She leaned back in the chair, her pale face marred by a cynicism new to its smooth planes. 'I went down to my mother's this weekend with the specific intention of breaking the news of the baby to them—only to have the wind taken out of my sails when they informed *me* th-that my mother is pregnant, too! And due to give birth at the same time!' Her voice was hoarse with too much emotion. Max had to look away. She let out another dull laugh. 'She feels a fool because she's thirty-eight years old and expecting, and I feel . . . '

She didn't finish—didn't need to. Max was learning more about her in these few tense hours than he had done in five months' intimacy with her. His mouth was drawn into a grim line, his expression dark and closed. Depression hung over them both and refused to allow the mood to lighten.

'So,' she continued on a sigh, 'I can look forward to becoming a sister at the same time as I make motherhood. And I mustn't, of course, forget my father's endowment policy—because, in all of this, that is the one good thing to come out of it. I will be financially secure!' Bitterness was welling up inside her again, and, though she tried to fight it, she had no success. 'That left only you to deal with, Max,' she said coldly. 'Have you any idea how predictable you are?' she taunted him, hating the way her heart enjoyed his discomfiture, the way the revealing flush skidded across his cheekbones. 'I knew from the moment I found out about the baby that you would think I'd done it on purpose. I could have predicted step by step your reaction, and you were good enough to prove me right . . . I had no intention of insisting you "do the right thing by me",' she mocked acidly. 'But I saw that you had a right to know, and——'

'Stop trying to play the bitch!' he exploded suddenly. 'It doesn't suit you. You're behaving like a child, and it——'

'But I *am* a child!' She came back with enough scorn to make him suck in his lips with barely controlled anger. "A child, who thought she could play grown-up games, and I got my just desserts for my arrogance.'

Max jerked out of the chair, muttering a few choice words beneath his breath as he slammed his coffee-cup down on the tray. His restlessness was back with a vengeance, she noted, as he began pacing the floor like a cat on the prowl.

He turned on her suddenly, anger in every line of his lean hard frame. 'Now you've got that little lot off your chest, do you think we could talk about the child and its future?' he drawled with more sarcasm than Clea had managed to achieve. 'I must presume that all that—waffling you've been doing for the past quarter of an hour was for the benefit of letting me know what a clever, independent little thing you are!' He sighed in an effort to control his temper, running a distracted hand through his dark hair and ruffling it out of its usual neatly groomed style. 'Yet in all these plans you've been making behind my damned back—I haven't heard you say one word about what you intend doing about the child! About my involvement in its upbringing and welfare. My right to some say in its destiny!' He glared at her for a second, then declared with husky verve, 'I don't want a child of mine growing up a bastard!'

The sheer cruelty of the word made her flinch. 'You didn't want to be a father, either,' she threw back hotly.

'And, if your claim of an accident is to be believed,' he

sliced, 'then you didn't want to be a mother. But the choice has been taken from *both* of us—*both of us,'* he repeated harshly. 'And that, in my book, leaves only one course left for us to take. We get married.'

Clea surged to her feet, facing him with a fury all of her own. 'You must think I'm crazy if you think I'll tie myself in marriage to a man who can't remain faithful for more than a few months!' she raged. It would be all too easy to give in to him. Max was stronger than her in every way, his arguments were stronger, his determination stronger, but she would not—could not give in on this point.

She saw, through her own anger, the lid once again lift off his. 'I never bloody touched her!' he shouted.

'But you were on the look-out for someone new!' she accused. 'If poor Dianne Stone wasn't it, then it would have been someone else. I'm not blind, Max!' she cried. 'You made very sure from the beginning that I understood the rules of the game. "No heavy commitment",' you said. "Just sex!" '

'No!' he growled, grabbing her shoulders and pulling her hard against him, his face tight with fury. 'That isn't true. You know there was more to us than just *sex!*'

'Do I?' Her soft mouth twisted in derision. 'It was all you ever wanted from me. You—you even cancelled last weekend because—because that commodity had been denied you! You took another woman to the theatre in my place. You said, "Poor Clea," ' she taunted recklessly, ' "you have a nice rest and I'll do the same." You—you even had the gall to come around here Friday night because she—she . . . '

What was she saying? Clea swayed within Max's grasp, shocked by the level of her bitterness. She was beginning to break up, she noted dazedly, her voice broken and bleeding as the bitter words poured out on a stunned Max.

'Clea, stop it! You'll make yourself ill!' he

muttered, watching as the whiteness returned to her face, his own expression fading from anger into concern. 'You have me all wrong! I don't see you as just a sex object! It would shame me to think I treated any woman that way—I—what's the use?' he sighed when he saw the disbelief on her face. 'You're a fool, Clea, if you can't see further than——'

'Yes, a fool,' she agreed thickly, cutting in on him because the close proximity of his body was turning hers to yearning jelly; his thighs tight against her thighs, his hard chest pressing against the heaving softness of her own.

She looked up at him with pained, appealing eyes, and the mood holding them changed, subtly shifting into the sensual. Max gazed down into her swimming eyes, and groaned hoarsely as his mouth softened and lowered on to hers. She met it, with her own lips parted and ready to receive him, her tongue slipping between his teeth to trace those sensitive areas within with an urgency born of fear. Her hands ran up the soft leather of his jacket and linked tightly around his neck, trembling fingers burying themselves into his hair, while Max pulled her closer to him, deepening the kiss with an urgent hunger of his own, his hands splaying over her arched back, moulding her to him so she could feel his instant, throbbing response to her closeness.

I love you, she told him with that kiss. Then, on a muffled sob, she broke away from him and crossed the room to lean against the sofa, struggling to find her composure.

'I won't marry you,' she stated thickly. 'You don't care for me enough for me to trust you, and I just couldn't cope with a life of not knowing whose bed you were warming when you weren't in mine. As for the baby . . .' She turned slowly to face him with a look of deadness in her eyes. 'You must do what you feel is right for you. I won't deny you your rights as a father, but as far as the rest goes——' she waved a heavy hand '—it's over. W-will you go now?' she appealed dully. 'I feel—tired.'

And she looked it—achingly so. Max stood looking at her for a long time, his gaze narrowed and sombre. He pushed his hands into his pockets and glanced broodingly at his feet for a moment, then nodded grimly.

'OK, we'll leave it for now,' he agreed quietly, and made for the door. 'Take care of yourself,' he added as he left her. 'I'll call you.'

Then he was gone. Max had a superb repertoire of exit lines. Clea had heard most of them, since she'd spent a lot of her time watching him walk out of her life.

CHAPTER EIGHT

BRAD GATTINGS was easy to work for. Clea's duties were by no means as interesting as they had been at the Computer Electronics Company, but the job filled a gap—served a purpose—even though there was a ganging up afoot to force her into giving up work altogether.

The pressures placed on her were consistent, and, for Clea, irritating. She didn't need to work. It was too hot. She should be resting more. She should be thinking of the baby's welfare, if she couldn't be bothered considering her own!

But she *liked* working! Brad was no hard taskmaster. After the complexities and pressures of working for Max, this job was a doddle by comparison. And Brad was always so easy-going with her. He didn't look grim-faced with censure every time he saw her—like some she could mention. He made her laugh, he would flirt with her unmercifully and make her feel like a woman instead of the huge balloon she resembled. He thought she looked sexy pregnant, not worn out! He thought there was something distinctly desirable about waist-length, gypsy-black hair and sexy long legs on a woman swollen with child. He said her face had a sultry kind of serenity about it that made him want to kiss it. No one should be allowed big pansy eyes like hers, and lips that naturally pouted invitation, while morally being unavailable. He didn't go on and on about her looking tired, wearied to death.

Max did. But then, Max was uncomfortable with her condition.

He refused to stop coming around to see her, but he didn't like it. He even insisted on taking her out regularly, for dinner somewhere, or to see a show, but she considered them *duty* excursions. And if he went out of his way to be kind and patient and very indulgent with her, then he also took great care to touch her as little as possible. Not that she wasn't relieved at this reticence. Every time his hand made contact with her arm, helping her in and out of his car, or just simply guiding her somewhere, her senses reacted like an alarm, painfully reminding her of what used to be. He hated looking at her, because she was carrying his child and he didn't want her to. He hadn't picked her out to be the mother of his children. He had picked her out to satisfy other much more basic needs. If she consented to marry him—and he had never given up suggesting it—he would have been bitterly regretting it by now, because sometimes he could barely stand looking at her—never mind living under the same roof as her! She had actually seen evidence of it in the tight pulling of his mouth when he thought she wasn't looking at him, or in the way he tensed up like piano-wire if she unintentionally brushed against him. His visits were kept up with the monotonous regularity that reminded her of hospital visits. A necessity that had to be endured.

Her mother wasn't much better. Although there was more genuine concern in Amy's manner, she just nagged too much. 'I rest for two hours every afternoon,' she repeatedly told Clea. 'And I have someone who does all my housework for me. London is just too hot for someone in our condition, I wish you would stop being so stubborn and move out of that flat. You could come and live here with us, then you would have both me and James. No worries at all, you wouldn't have to do a jot if you didn't want to!'

James would sometimes turn up at lunch time and drag her out to some exclusive restaurant, sitting over her while she ate. He would frown and look concerned, tell her she wasn't eating properly, that she looked pale and drawn when she thought she looked and felt fine! Once he'd gone away again, however, she *would* be feeling decidedly haggard!

And now her doctor had joined in the fray. 'You aren't taking those iron tablets regularly.' Max would appreciate that, thought Clea wryly, she was lousy at taking pills. 'Your blood pressure is up—not much—but up. I think it's time you stopped working. This hot weather saps your energy. You're carrying around extra weight you aren't used to. The baby needs sustenance to develop, which it takes from you, and therefore leaves you tired sooner than you expect. You should give up your job.'

Only Brad abstained from nagging. But then, he had purely selfish reasons to keep her sweet, since he was relying on her work until his secretary got back from her travels. She knew she was indispensable to Brad, but at least he didn't nag!

The situation with Max was the one that caused her the most irritation. It hadn't been easy to convince him that she had meant what she'd said that awful night. And he had maintained a steady pressure on her ever since to change her mind. His moods, at first, had alternated between the downright bullying to the coolly resolute, placing arguments before her that she sometimes found difficult to fight. 'I have a beautiful home on the Devonshire coast,' he'd told her only a few weeks ago, when the heatwave had struck. 'The air there is so fresh and clean. And my mother would love having you stay there, Clea. You need a holiday before the baby is born, or you won't be fit to take care of him when he does arrive. Just a fortnight, Clea!' he'd gone on to urge when he caught her wistful expression. 'Think of it as an annual holiday. Everyone needs one, including you.'

Now that had been tempting, she had to admit. But the idea of meeting his mother, and worse, giving her aching heart memories of yet another side to Max, hardened her against it. 'I can't let Brad down,' she insisted stubbornly. 'He needs me until September. I'll have a whole month, then, to rest before the baby.'

But sometimes, when she was alone in her flat, and her emotions found a crack by which to escape and haunt her, she would wonder how different things would be if she gave in to Max's pressure, maybe even married him. To be cosseted like her mother, cared for by Max—even if it was an unloving Max. Ah, but those low times were hard to bear, and her heart would squeeze in lonely yearning as an image of him would float up in front of her—the other Max, the one with the smile that devastated, or just the tall, lean shape of him, naked, tanned skin gleaming with the sheen of recent loving, limbs tangled with her own. Memories like those were severely cut out. Because she no longer had the right to recall them. She had given it away the night she had told him she was pregnant.

And so he continued to visit her, take her out, lavish the force of his personality on her, while she determinedly rebuffed him. Recently a new mood had crept up on them, a mood of ruthless civility that was, in actual fact, a slow-burning cauldron of resentments. And one day, she knew, it was all going to bubble over.

And then what? she wondered. She didn't know; she wasn't even sure who was causing the resentment. All she did know was that she wasn't going to put herself in the position of being married to a man who could only manage to feel *fond* of her.

Fond. What a pathetic word! She was *fond* of Italian ice-cream, but she could live quite happily without it. Fond! He had no idea how utterly desperate she'd felt when he'd applied that word to her!

So, they had continued through the last months in a guarded kind of affability that scorned what they had once shared. The larger Clea's body got, the sharper became the edge of her tongue. And the more she found she could say to him without receiving any healthy retaliation, the more she tried his control. It was a petty way of getting back at him, she knew, but it didn't stop her using it. It was hard to hold back on the bitterness when her heart was broken—silly, foolish heart that had never been invited to love the man it had chosen. Max didn't want her love. He didn't want her to have his baby. He just accepted the situation with good, if grim, grace; she had to give him that, if nothing else. He had refused to give up on her when, deep down, she knew it was what she deserved.

The telephone rang on Monday morning, just as Clea was getting ready to go for her monthly check-up with her gynaecologist.

'Hello?' she mumbled, sounding breathless, struggling as she was to fasten the bib buckles on her pale aqua-blue cotton dungarees which had suddenly become too tight.

'Clea, I caught you, then!' It was her mother, sounding superbly fit and not even a little breathless. 'What are you doing?'

'Trying to dress myself while talking to you,' she replied wryly, the phone tucked under her chin. 'I have an appointment at the doctor's in half an hour.'

'Oh—I won't keep you, then,' Amy said, picking up on Clea's brisk tone. 'Remember to tell him about the slight swell-ing around your ankles.'

'Yes, Mummy.' It was the heat that Clea blamed, but

she didn't feel like joining in one of her mother's long discussions on pregnancy, so she kept her reply to its briefest.

'. . . And the tiredness, mention the tiredness.'

The tiredness had been a silly mistake on her part when she had stupidly fallen asleep at dinner last night in front of her mother and James. They had been furious, blaming her job, as usual. James all but threw her into his car and drove her home. He even stayed while she showered and got into bed! They hadn't given her a chance to explain how she'd hardly slept a wink the night before because the baby had spent the night kicking her to death!

'Yes, Mummy,' she meekly replied again. 'What did you ring for, exactly?'

'Oh, yes . . .' Amy sounded disconcerted, she wasn't used to her daughter's meek obedience. 'A party, here, on Saturday next. Can you come? It will probably be the last time James and I entertain on any real level before the baby. James thinks it will become too much for me. You could come Saturday morning and stay overnight as you usually do when you come down. James will drive you back home Sunday. It could be fun, what do you think?'

Clea heaved a sigh of relief as the bib buckle slid home. 'It sounds nice. Thank you, I'd love to come.'

'Good,' said a pleased Amy. 'How is the weather affecting you? James tells me London is steaming. It isn't so bad out here where the air is a lot fresher. I can't believe the summer could be so cruel as to keep this heatwave up for a whole six weeks, while I'm the size of a house. You would think it would show some consideration!'

'Amen to that,' agreed Clea with verve. It was mid-July and the sun had shone constantly since the beginning of June. 'And I'm going to have to buy myself some new clothes,' she added absently, looking ruefully down at the dungarees that fitted across her middle far more tightly than they were supposed to fit. 'I've got the whole morning off, so I think I'll do a bit of shopping after the doctor's—I'll buy something nice for Saturday!' she decided brightly. 'Which reminds me, I *have* to go!'

The telephone began ringing a second time as she was about to leave the flat. She considered ignoring it, before flouncing over to answer it when her curiosity got too much for her.

'Clea? Don't you have an appointment with your gynaecologist today?'

'I was just on my way out of the door to keep it,' she informed her caller impatiently. She had screwed up her hair in a knot on top of her head because its heavy weight irritated her, now the pins were sticking in her scalp to further annoy her. This, on top of everything else, made her sound truculent. 'What do you want, Max? I'm going to be late.' He sounded cool and energetic. She could actually imagine the efficient air-conditioning in his office keeping him cool. It wasn't fair, but then, it didn't take much for her to feel hostile towards Max.

'I thought you might like a lift to work afterwards,' he offered levelly, taking no notice of her ill-mannered tone. 'It's so hot out there that the concrete is beginning to crack. Tell me what time you're due out and I'll meet you.'

'Thanks, but no thanks,' she refused tersely, angered for some reason at his calm supposition that she would fall in with his plans. 'I'm not going back to the office directly from the doctor's.' She hated having to explain her movements, for it invariably led to criticism. So her voice had a defiant tinge to it. 'I'm going shopping—for some new clothes.'

'Not in this heat, you're not!' came the anticipated cry. Here we go again, she thought, looking painfully at the ceiling. 'Why can't you use one of those special designer places where they send out a selection of clothes to suit

your size that you can try on at leisure in your own home?
I can't see . . .'

Her temper snapped, making her cut in ruthlessly on
him, her tongue as sharp as a razor. 'Because that kind of
service costs vast amounts of money. And I don't happen
to have vast amounts!'

'If you would only climb down off your high principles
and accept my help, you can afford anything you damned
well please!'

'Accept your *conscience money*, you mean?' As soon as
she'd said it, Clea was appalled at herself. That was most
definitely the worst thing she had ever said to him.

The silence hummed in her ears, and she chewed
uncomfortably on her bottom lip while Max, she was sure,
simmered in his air-conditioned office. Then she heard a
long and heavy sigh, and winced visibly at it.

'Do you know, Clea . . .' His voice was low and grim. 'I
never thought I could ever actively dislike you, but
sometimes I come very close to it.'

The line went dead and she stood, holding the receiver
for a long moment afterwards, feeling utterly ashamed of
herself.

'. . . You either slow down, young lady,' Dr Fielding
pointed a threatening pen at a subdued Clea, 'or I'll have
you admitted to hospital, where they'll *make* you
rest—understand?'

Clea nodded mutely.

'Heatwaves like this one have seen healthier pregnant
women than you flat on their backs with exhaustion.'

He studied her downbent head, following the soft curve
of her cheek and jaw—and smiled drily to himself. She
possessed the most astounding beauty. And pregnancy
suited her, it exposed a little of that extra dimension she
would normally keep hidden. The warmer Latin side . . .

Whoever the man was who had passed her over must be a blind fool. For Clea Maddon was of those rare woman who would only improve with age. She brightened his day, just sitting here.

'. . . Feet up on something whenever you sit down—and do that often, to ease the pressure on those ankles. And do you think you could *try* to take your iron tablets every day?' He didn't sound optimistic. And the guilty grin Clea sent made him sigh, half in exasperation, half in defeat. It was too hot, she was just too pretty, and his weary old senses were simply captivated by that smile—so full of guile, full of impertinent charm.

'Oh—off you go!' he dismissed ruefully. 'But I want to see you again in two weeks—*two weeks*, mind! And before that if you suffer from any light-headedness or signs of giddiness.'

Clea came down the surgery steps, smiling to herself at the doctor's fatherly admonishments. He really was a dear old thing. But he didn't seem to understand that she felt so well! The sun was shining—and the sky was a beautiful unblemished blue! Her baby was slumbering for a brief while, and so not pummelling her. And she was off on a shopping spree!

It was with that smile presented to the sun that Max first glimpsed her, and it held him caught for a long and breathless moment before he opened the car door and slowly climbed out, his narrowed gaze taking in every detail of her.

She had no idea how enchanting she looked in those ridiculous baggy dungarees. Tall and graceful, even while the evidence of her pregnancy pushed determinedly at the pale aqua-blue cloth. Her feet were pushed into canvas slip-ons' of a matching colour, and she had a large matching canvas bag slung over one shoulder. Her eyes were shining with a love of life that hadn't been there for some months. Her hair—that glorious mass of gleaming black silk—had been coiled in a tight knot on top of her well shaped head, leaving vulnerable the gentle curve of cheek and long creamy neck. She looked young, contented and beautiful. The vision tugged at the lines of his mouth as he gripped the rim of the open car door.

'Clea!'

The call brought her head swinging around in his direction. She stood stiff and straight, her feet placed slightly apart, tummy sticking out in an unconscious balancing of weight. Purple eyes squinted into the bright sunlight, a frown marring her smooth brow. Then surprise showed on her face.

'Want a lift?' Max offered, searching for a smile and finding it in the half-twist of his attractive mouth.

He looked clean and alive: his black hair blowing a little in the gentle warmth of the summer breeze, lean face a perfect fashioning of hard bone and smooth, tanned skin that helped make him the very attractive man he was. He wasn't wearing a jacket, it was just too hot for City convention. Even the most staid City gents had resorted to walking around jacketless this summer. Max had gone one step further and removed his tie also, loosening the top few buttons on his shirt; the crisp white cotton clung to his broad frame as if to deliberately draw attention to the taut dark skin beneath where the mat of masculine body hair showed as a sensual shadow against the clean cotton.

Clea's cheeks began to warm with a guilty flush—because of what she'd said on the phone earlier, and because an unbidden surge of awareness was suddenly affecting her blood pressure. How do I combat that, Dr Fielding? she queried silently. By not looking at Max, when my eyes want to hungrily eat him up? By pretending my traitorous body doesn't intimately remember how wonderful he feels when clamped sensuously to me? How do I combat his effect on me when the mere sight of him sends my blood pressure soaring?

She hadn't actually expected to see him for at least a week. On other times when she'd behaved rather badly to him, Max had gone into recluse for a while, as if to give her, as well as himself, time to get over the bitterness that would well up. He'd broken the rules this time by turning up here, and her soft mouth pouted unconsciously while she tried to decide how best to approach this surprise situation.

Then, with a pert uplifting of her chin, Clea spun on her heel and walked slowly towards him and his low, black, growling monster of a car.

'Has that thing got air-conditioning?' she enquired, to hide her embarrassment. She hadn't liked herself very much since this morning's altercation.

He smiled, coming around the car to lean easily against the long, low bonnet. 'If it hasn't,' he drawled with a touch of wry amusement, 'then Aston Martin need suing.' The car was brand new. He had only picked it up the day before. 'I didn't pay out the exorbitant fee this thing cost to get only half a car.'

'Whew, it's hot,' she sighed as she reached him, hiding her discomfort behind a feigned airiness, handing him her canvas bag as though it were the natural thing to do— not that the bag was heavy, there was hardly anything in it. It was just the heat getting to her, and Max. She smiled shyly up at him, still flushed, her expression becoming contrite. 'I'm sorry for what I said this morning,' she apologised gruffly, deciding to get it over with. His eyes were warm on her, dark and smoky. She hadn't seen them so unguarded for months. 'I was in a rush, and my mother had just rung off after issuing one of her lectures. I'm afraid you caught me at a bad moment.'

Her bag dangled from his hooked fingers by its aqua-blue straps. Why she had handed him her bag she had no idea, she certainly wouldn't have dared doing such a thing at one time. Yet he didn't seem bothered. He was smiling.

'Then, in future, I'll enquire if you've spoken to your mother *before* I start to nag!' He was looking at her with laughter in his eyes, trying to make her comfortable, telling her he understood, when really she didn't understand herself why she had attacked him like that.

She shifted uneasily, feeling a little overawed by this softer, more indulgent Max. He looked what he was, a successful man of business, a man who was comfortable in luxury and elegance. Clea carried no social chips on her shoulder, yet he managed to make her feel a trifle inadequate at this moment.

Oh, what the heck! she thought on a burst of happiness. The sun was shining, and she was experiencing a delicious contentment with life. Max was here, and *he* looked happy . . . She lifted her face up to his, and beamed him a smile that wrinkled her small nose with a touch of that same impishness the doctor had enjoyed earlier.

'I'm off to buy some clothes that fit!' she claimed, with only a touch of defiance in her purple gaze.

He ran his gaze mockingly over her, eyes glinting when he saw the return of her blush. 'I rather like it,' he announced with a smile. 'You look sort of—clownish. All baggy pants and beaming face. I like it.'

'Clownish!' Clea repeated in affront. 'You think I look *clownish*?'

'An endearing clown,' he assured teasingly, his chest heaving on an uplift of spirit.

The sun shone down on them, and perhaps it was its doing that they both experienced a warmth inside as well as out—or perhaps it was because, at last, the tension between them was beginning to evaporate.

Maybe she had needed to say something truly hurtful to snap her out of the bitter hostility she had felt towards him. Or maybe time did heal a little, and she was at last finding it in her heart to forgive him. Whatever, there was a definite shift in the mood between them, and it was a relief to feel it so.

As if he couldn't resist the need, Max reached out with a finger to trail it slowly down one of her flushed cheeks. 'Hello,' he said huskily.

'Hello,' Clea returned. Why, neither knew, except that the greeting seemed to announce the acceptance of some new fragile, if elusive, terms between them.

They stared mutely at one another for a long moment, then Max sucked in a deep breath and let it slowly out again. 'Shopping?'

Clea nodded. 'New clothes for the fat lady.'

He took her arm and guided her to the passenger door of the car, helping her inside. 'New clothes for the fat lady,' he repeated, with tongue-in-cheek solemnity.

It was only as they were driving along that an idea hit her, and Clea turned to look speculatively at him. 'Are you actually considering coming shopping with me?' she enquired curiously.

His mouth twitched, his quick glance in her direction full of teasing charm. 'I'm very good at choosing clothes for fat ladies,' he assured her.

Clea laughed, but didn't really believe him. 'You can't spare the time—and you know it.' She, above anyone, knew how hard Max had to work daily just to keep on top of things at the office.

'And you forget that I'm the boss,' he pointed out. 'I can do anything I damned well please. And I fancy shopping with you,' he added, with some of his usual arrogance. 'After all—who is there to sack me for playing truant?'

'No one,' she mocked. 'No one would dare! You'd probably have them assassinated if they tried!'

'You do have a low opinion of me,' Max observed, with more candour than amusement. 'How about you playing truant with me—and I'll throw in lunch as a bonus for good behaviour . . . surely if my company can survive without its chairman for a day, Gattings can survive the same without his secretary?'

Clea thought about it. The whole thing was getting a bit bizarre. It was one thing to attempt burying the hatchet, but quite another to allow her guard to slip too far where Max was concerned. She had never known him to be quite so approachable. There was something decidedly fishy about his attitude, and yet, it was nice. It tugged at that thin thread of need she had where he was concerned. Could one day hurt her that much? Yes, a small voice replied. It could hurt a great deal.

'OK.' She threw all warnings to the wind and smiled at Max. 'Find me a phone, so I can tell Brad that the doctor insists I rest, and we'll shop together—with lunch thrown in,' she reminded him firmly.

His gaze sharpened. 'And did he—tell you to rest?' he enquired with studied lightness.

Clea wagged a finger at him in a fair mimic of the doctor's pen-wagging gesture. 'Slow down, young lady—or I'll hospitalise you!' She shrugged carelessly unaware of her companion's sudden gravity. 'He doesn't seem to understand that I feel so well! What with my mother, James, the doctor—and *you*, all lecturing me, I feel suffocated by overconcern sometimes. Only Brad treats me like a normal human being. Thank God! I think I'd go a little mad if he started nagging, too.'

She watched Max automatically stiffen at the mention

of Brad Gattings. He didn't like the man, he had told her often enough. He considered Brad a womaniser, and *she* considered his criticism hilarious since, to her, he was only describing himself! A bit like the pot calling the kettle black!

'The trouble with Gattings is, he neither knows nor cares what's good for you,' Max muttered as they drove on. 'He'd use that charm of his on any beautiful woman—if it meant him getting what he needed from her.'

'Are you insinuating that Brad——'

'No,' he cut in curtly, anticipating her. 'He's not so stupid as to burn his boats where you're concerned while you're so indispensable to him.'

The tension was back, like little invisible devils, flitting between them, prodding them both with barbed forks.

'Like you did, you mean,' she muttered.

The silence was uncomfortable; they drove for quite a while before Max replied, and when he did, Clea jumped nervously.

'I won't let you set me up, Clea,' he warned softly, his meaning quite clear. 'I've got your measure now, so be warned. I won't take the flak from your sanctimonious gun any more.'

Sanctimonious! 'I don't know what you mean,' she denied offishly, oddly discomfited by his choice of word, because she was certain Max had chosen it carefully.

'Yes, you do,' he stated quietly. 'So just be careful from now on, sweetheart, because you may find yourself in too deep if you try pitting those vicious wits against mine from now on.'

Clea frowned. He was challenging her for some reason known only to himself. It sent a warning shiver down her spine. Max had come out of hiding, she realised uncomfortably. She wasn't sure that she liked the idea.

CHAPTER NINE

SURPRISINGLY, Clea did enjoy the day, and by the time Max drew up outside her flat, she was at peace with him, enough to invite him in for coffee.

Max carried in the mounds of packages she had accumulated during the day, his expression still rueful at the amount of shopping a woman could pack into a few hours. They'd eaten lunch in a nice French restaurant, lingering over coffee because they'd been talking intently over some subject that, now, Clea couldn't bring back to mind. If she was honest, Max had made a surprising impact on her today. Oh, not in the old way—that had never really disappeared, anyway—no, he had actually impressed her with the serious and thinking side of his character. She had seen this side of him while working for him, of course, but never outside the office. She had once wondered if he ever did use his intelligence in any other way than on the problems of computer technology. Now she knew he did.

'My mother wants to meet you,' he announced blandly on walking into the kitchen, after ridding himself of her packages. 'And I think it's time I met your family.'

Clea didn't reply immediately, appearing to be busy with the coffee-maker, and loading the tray. She had this unreasonable dread of meeting his mother. Clea felt sure she must be some kind of paragon to have mothered a son like Max—the arrogance and assertiveness had to come from somewhere, didn't it?

'Don't misunderstand me,' he went on, after watching

her troubled face for a while. 'I haven't put the marriage idea away. I just think that this—this stalemate we've been locked in through the last months should come to an end, and be resolved before the baby is born. It seems a good beginning, to get to know our respective families. They will, after all, be playing an important role in the baby's life.' His blue eyes studied her elusive ones with an unswerving steadiness.

Finding herself on the defensive, Clea shrugged. 'I don't see how meeting my——'

'Now, let's just get one thing straight,' he cut in grimly. A gap of a good two yards separated them, but she suddenly felt under attack. He pointed a warning finger at her. 'I won't be cut out of this baby's life. I won't be consigned to the role of intruder, just because you think you have all the answers neatly slotted into their correct boxes—which puts me in the one marked "Louse".' Clea flinched. 'At the moment, I can see no solution, other than playing this thing the way you've decided it has to be played, since you seem to hold all the most important cards—the delicacy of your condition being the main one, because it stops me from forcing any issue you feel sensitive about, in case I upset you too much . . .'

'It's not a game, Max,' she cut in derisively.

'You're dead right!' he grated. 'It's not. It may do you well to remember that. As I was saying . . .' He took in a controlled breath, as though trying to curb a desire to snarl, while she stood, blinking at the rebuke. 'I have had to come to terms with the fact that you don't see me as good husband material.' He threw back her own words from months ago, with notable contempt. 'Now you have to come to terms with the fact that I will *not* be pushed rudely to the sidelines of my child's existence. So, we'll start by laying the foundations, upon which to build some kind of working relationship that will be acceptable to both of us. Beginning with a meeting of our respective families.'

Clea made a play of sorting out the tray, hurt that he should now be wishing to take an interest in her family, for the baby's sake, when he hadn't bothered to do so for herself alone.

'Fair enough,' she conceded on a small shrug, then came back with her own little dig, 'Of course, I can't guarantee that my parents will want to meet you.' She felt a sting of satisfaction when his face stiffened. 'But I'll speak to them, see if I can arrange a night when we can go over there for dinner . . .'

'No.' He threw her into confused silence by shaking his head, then took her by surprise by smiling ruefully. 'If you don't mind,' he murmured. 'I would rather meet them on my own ground. I'd prefer to give them dinner, at my apartment.'

'Ah.' Once again Clea felt the hurt he had unwittingly inflicted on her. She had never been honoured with a visit to his apartment. In all those months of close intimacy, Max had never taken her there, never allowed her to cross that invisible line drawn for mistresses. Now he was blandly removing the barrier—for the baby's sake—for appearance's sake—for his own conscience's sake! 'Then I'm sure they will be suitably—impressed,' she clipped, moving at last from the stiff position she had held since the conversation had begun.

I wish I smoked, she thought desperately. I need something to numb the nerves just now. The day had gone so well, too! Now he was spoiling it, and deliberately, she thought.

'Look——' His tone changed, became heavy. 'You gave clear guidelines on how I'm allowed to behave in this—this——'

'Mess!' she bit out, then turned angrily on him, her

hands gripping the worktop, while her eyes flashed with unusual fury. 'Will you stop talking to me as though I were just another statistic in your damned computerlike mind?'

He looked taken aback, his head held haughtily as he stared at her. 'I'm sorry,' he murmured gruffly. 'I didn't mean to——'

'Oh, you never *mean* to do anything, do you, Max?' she said scornfully, banging mugs on to a tray. 'You never meant to complicate your life with an unwanted baby! You never meant to make me feel cheap, dirty, underhand! You never meant to get yourself in this—distasteful position in the first place! It isn't your fault!' she cried, flushed now, in full aggrieved flow. 'So here we are, discussing the solutions your damned logical brain has come up with to an—illogical situation! And you actually expect me to comply!'

'Put that milk jug down,' he said quietly, eyeing her warily, 'before you drop it.'

Clea stared blankly at the small white china jug in her hand, and was amazed to see how much she was trembling. Her whole body was shaking: hands, arms, body, legs. On a flash of sheer, blinding fury she lifted her hand and took aim.

Even as she threw the jug, and watched it flying in a topsy-turvy fashion towards Max's head, she was shocked at her own loss of control, stunned to find she was actually capable of reacting so childishly.

It missed, but only because Max ducked, and the jug splintered against the wall behind him, shattering into a thousand tinkling fragments to the tiled floor.

They stood, staring at each other, the jug ignored now as silence of a violent kind filled the space around them. Max was as shocked as she. He was looking at her as though seeing a stranger, a rather dangerous stranger.

'What the hell's the matter with you?' he suddenly

exploded. 'What the hell is it you *want* from me?'

'Nothing!' she all but screamed at him. 'I want absolutely nothing from you.' Her mouth wanted to turn down in a sneer, but it ended up quivering with an onset of tears instead, her eyes stinging hotly. 'You want to meet my family? OK, I'll arrange it!' she cried wildly, hands flailing, body shaking so much it affected her voice. 'You want to play the responsible father? I won't stop you! But don't you *dare* come in here—into my home, spouting out commands at me, treating me like one of your damned employees who's—who's turned temperamental on you. You know nothing about me, do you?' she went on thickly, while the coffee-maker blubbed and popped, and Max stood, pinned to the spot by her hysterical outburst. 'What I think, feel, like and don't like? You know I'm good in bed,' she sneered at him. 'You're probably even quite proud of how well you taught me in that area. You know I can type a neat letter, answer a telephone, make—make your damned coffee——' Her hand made an uncontrollable swipe at the glass coffee-maker, only by sheer bad aim missing sending the whole lot, boiling coffee and all, flying like the fated jug. 'Just how you damned well like it! There he stands!' She sent that same hand flailing in his direction in a scornful gesture. 'Mr God Almighty Max Latham! God's gift to women and computers! So—so damned wrapped up in himself and his own importance that he can't see past his own ego!' He went to speak, but Clea glared him into silence, bending towards him slightly, hands on hips, like a shrew. 'I'm not playing the martyr! I'm not being oh, so damned self-righteous by refusing your so-called offer! I know exactly what I was to you—and what a damned bloody mess I've put that neat and tidy life of yours in! So don't come in here, spouting nice brisk platitudes at me to prove how honourable you are—how responsible! I find it insulting to my intelligence! You don't need me, Max! Or this baby! And I won't become an ever-grateful weight around your neck, just to appease your feelings of guilt because you happened to realise that I wasn't deliberately trying to threaten your precious freedom!'

What was she saying? She came to a halt as abruptly as she had flared up. Max, white-faced and stance as taut as a bow-string, stared at her for long excruciating seconds, a warning nerve twitching at the corner of his clenched jaw.

She stood, holding her breath, fatally aware that retribution was well overdue. Her unruly tongue had been given too much leeway recently, it seemed to have forgotten how to keep still.

The inevitable came, with two giant strides from those long legs that brought him up against her trembling body. His hands came up to grasp her upper arms, they gave a vicious tug, and she found herself flattened, baby and all, up against the rock-hard length of his furious frame.

'You asked for this,' he hissed, just before his head came down and took her mouth in a bruising kiss meant to punish.

Her mind went into a spin, shock mingling with the injection of a fierce awareness of his body that made her groan against his mouth. It had been so long—so long since they'd kissed—that even this punishing embrace was like a banquet to her starved senses.

'Max——' She tried to free her mouth, fighting both him and herself.

'You're so beautiful!' he choked, refusing to let her go. but the kiss altered, became softer and more coaxing. 'So damned beautiful. How the hell have I kept my hands off you for so long?'

He glared down at her pale face for a moment, as if wishing her to the devil, then he was brushing light, enticing kisses along her upper lip, touching his tongue to the sensitive corners of her mouth, dragging from her a soft sigh of pleasure. His hands slackened and became caressing. Clea clung shamefully to him, unable to find the strength to push him away. It had always been like this for her: one touch from him and she was his slave. And there lay the reason for all her hostility, she noted tragically. She had always known that to let him get this close would mean disaster.

'Max . . .' she murmured, when he eventually allowed her to speak. 'About what I just said . . . I'm sorry. I shouldn't have said it.'

He straightened a little, but didn't let her go, his hands light on her shoulderblades. 'Why not—if you meant it?' His kiss-softened mouth twisted. 'You don't like me very much, do you?' he added with bitter wryness.

Clea shook her head mutely. Liking had never come into her feelings for him.

'One hell of a mess,' he murmured softly.

'One hell of a mess,' she ruefully agreed.

She wanted to move away, break contact with him, but her defences had tumbled, and she found herself in desperate need of this small physical contact just now. Max seemed to understand, because he held her like that for a long while before gently putting her away from him.

'The—the coffee,' she stammered nervously.

'I don't want any now, thanks,' drawled Max, as though amused by the suggestion. He moved towards the kitchen door, turning to look at her once his hand had made contact with the doorhandle. 'Have dinner with me tomorrow night?'

Clea stiffened, taken by surprise. She hadn't expected him to want see her again so soon after . . . 'I don't think . . .'

'I'll revise that remark,' he cut in drily. 'You *will* have dinner with me tomorrow night, Clea,' he stated arrogantly. 'And in the mean time you can think about how best we can arrange to meet your family. I'll see you about seven, tomorrow night. Bye for now.'

And he was gone, with one of his usual impeccable exit lines, leaving her feeling ever so slightly bemused.

Why had that happened? Clea found herself puzzling later that night. And, more to the point, why had Max let it happen? She could excuse herself, because her own feelings had always been more deeply involved than his had ever been. Yet Max had deliberately set out to knock her off guard today. Every word and gesture had been carefully produced to make her sit up and take notice of him, realise that he was determined to show a different side to himself. For what end?

She didn't know, but spent most of that night and the following day worrying over it, until her mind whirled with the effort, and was in the end no closer to fathoming him out.

By the time seven o'clock came around, she was in a high state of nervous tension. Another blisteringly hot day hadn't helped her find her usual calm, nor had a sudden rush at the office when a late consignment of software came in, and had to be immediately dished out to frantically screaming customers.

The doorbell went dead on time. Clea muttered something derogatory beneath her breath and went to answer it. 'Whoever designed this dress forgot to allow for the handicaps of pregnancy,' she grumbled, not even looking at Max before she was turning away from him to walk back down the hall, struggling irritably with the back zip on her new white voile dress. 'I can't do it!' she sighed, dropping her hands so they hung tensely by her sides, her face a picture of frustration as she turned to face him again. 'My hair's a mess, my dress won't fasten—and I'm sure I've put on two stone since I bought this thing!' She gave the lovely white cloth an impatient tug. 'I don't think I want to go out, after all.'

Max swallowed a smile; he was sensitive enough to know Clea wouldn't appreciate it at this moment. His gaze ran over her, enjoying the picture she made, with her skin glowing from a recent shower and smelling of that elusive scent he always associated with Clea. No make-up, it was just too hot for sticky cosmetics and she didn't need them. Her hair has been recently washed, too, and shone with health and vitality. She looked absolutely beautiful, the new dress an exquisitely designed fall of fine white pleats from a wide-yoked collar that curved her slender throat and lay flat against her skin all the way to the full swell of her breasts—or would do, he amended wryly, if the dress was zipped properly.

'Turn around,' he told her drily. She was pouting like a petulant child, just asking to be kissed into good humour. 'I can easily do up your dress. Your hair is lovely—all wild and free, just how I like it. You haven't put on any weight whatsoever, you're just fed-up, that's all, and most probably hungry. The weather is too hot, and you work too hard, so you're tired and tetchy. Now turn around.'

Clea looked, actually looked at him for the first time. It was his indulgent manner that made her take notice of him, but it was his appearance that held her suddenly breathless. She had never seen him dressed so beautifully casual before, in cream silk shirt and caramel coloured trousers that lay flat against his lean hips, the light material faithfully following the long powerful lines of his legs.

'Taking me to McDonalds?' she quipped, to hide her sudden agitation.

His twisting smile was appreciative of the jibe. 'No,' he replied glibly, waiting for her to turn so he could zip up her dress, while she was reluctant to let him.

She didn't want Max seeing her naked back, she didn't want him to learn just how altered her body was since he'd looked on it last. Her eyes went wide as she stared mutely up at him, and in the end Max sighed mockingly and stepped around behind her. Her fingers clutched at the two pieces of material. Max prised them away with firm gentle hands.

'Stop it,' he said when she stiffened at the first touch of his fingers against her heated skin. 'I've seen you in less . . . Here.' He twisted her hair into one thick tress and passed it to her over her shoulder. 'Hang on to this.'

Clea hung on—like a lifeline, breath suspended as those tormenting fingers brushed upwards along her spine, drawing the zip with them.

'There,' he murmured. 'Ordeal over.' He reclaimed her hair, and Clea shut her eyes tightly on a release of tension—then was taken completely by surprise when she felt the warm touch of his mouth against her exposed nape. It was barely there before it was gone, too brief an intrusion for her to have time to protest, and her hair was being carefully arranged about her shoulders.

'Let's go,' he said huskily.

It was quite hot outside, the sun still high enough to make Clea blink as she stepped out into it. So maybe it was the glare of the sun that could be blamed for what happened next, or maybe some of the blame could be because of the deep sense of disappointment she found herself struggling with at Max's deft defusing of a tense situation.

She didn't see or hear the two young teenagers racing towards her on skateboards. It was only the quick reaction of the man behind her that saved her from a potentially serious accident. Max's arms whipped around her midsection, dragging her back against him as first one boy

then the other whizzed madly by. Her shocked surprise
transferred itself to her baby and he kicked out in protest,
causing Max to start as the kick thumped against his
splayed palm.

It was sheer reaction that made him snatch his hand
away, but Clea couldn't stop the embarrassed blush from
staining her cheeks, and she moved shakily away from
him, going to stand by the car while Max followed at a
slower pace. He was pale, his face drawn into troubled
lines.

Clea felt a pang of sympathy for him. How different
things would have been had they been in love and looking
forward together to the birth of their first child. Max had
just experienced, for the first time, the living movement of
his own creation inside her womb. For any normal father
this would have been an uplifting experience, but for Max?
Whatever he was feeling, she thought gravely, he was
doing so deeply. Sad, that he couldn't show it. And she
knew her sympathy to be well placed, for, whatever else
she regretted about her association with Max, she would
never regret having his child.

'Where are we eating?' she asked, breaking into the
silence filling the small confines of the car, and watching
him covertly.

'What?' He sounded far away, his expression wearing
that glazed look of grim thoughtfulness. 'Oh . . .' They
were heading towards Knightsbridge. 'A surprise.' He
managed a teasing smile for her, but it was a little strained.

Clea tried again. 'Well,' she exclaimed lightly. 'You're
certainly not dressed for the Ritz!'

'Does it hurt?'

'What?' It was her turn to sound surprised.

'When he kicks like that,' Max explained huskily,
throwing a quick frowning glance at her, 'does it hurt?'

Clea sucked in a controlled breath. He wasn't enquiring

out of bland curiosity; he was concerned, really concerned. 'Sometimes,' she answered wryly. 'But most of the time I find the experience—comforting.' It was difficult to put into words something that was essentially a spiritual thing. 'I would be more concerned if he didn't move. But, yes, sometimes the movement can press on a nerve or accidentally kick out at something painful.'

'I apologise for reacting the way I did.'

'There's no need. I understood.'

'No, you didn't,' he muttered roughly. 'You couldn't possibly understand.'

She opened her mouth to demand he explain that last remark. It had been said with a touch of derision aimed directly at her—but Max cut in on her, effectively killing the subject. 'We're here,' he said, and diverted her by turning the car into a narrow driveway leading to a car park belonging to a block of residential apartments. The area was vaguely familiar to Clea, but she couldn't recall there being a restaurant around here.

He reversed the car into a slot between a Mercedes and a Rolls Royce, then killed the engine, sitting back in his seat and turning to look at her.

'My apartment,' he told her levelly.

CHAPTER TEN

CLEA slid her gaze towards the impressive brick building.

Max's apartment was on the fourth storey, covering the whole floor. Six bay windows—she counted them carefully, three to one side of the central lift shaft, three to the other. Did a couple of those bays belong to Mr and Mrs Walters, who looked after him? Or did Max command the whole floor to himself? He owned the whole building, Clea knew, because during the course of her duties while working for him, she had done correspondence for him regarding the other leases.

She was unsure as to why she was concentrating her whole attention on these unimportant facts, when the situation was so unprecedented that she should be concerning herself with questioning his motives for bringing her here.

He sat very still beside her, watching her, those guarded blue eyes studying her reaction.

'Dinner,' he said quietly. 'Prepared by Mrs Walters for us to share in comfort.'

Of course, she thought, and turned an expressionless face to him. 'Because your invitation to my parents made you realise it may look odd if my first time here should happen to correspond with theirs?'

His wicked grin refused the offer of another row. 'Or maybe because I plan to have my evil way with your body,' he leered.

'What—this body?' Clea's own sense of humour asserted itself, showing in an affected amazement. 'No

130

way!' She shook her head. 'No way could you convince me you wanted *this* body.'

They were still smiling and joking lightly as they left the lift on the top floor. But all traces of laughter died, as Clea came to an abrupt halt at the surprise that met her in what must be a private foyer to the three flat doors leading off from it.

Eyes wide, she stared at walls of bright white. Furniture of a Chinese dynasty—black lacquered and imposing—and splashes of yellow on modern abstract paintings in black frames, should have looked out of place, yet managed to blend with the purely aggressive surroundings. For a mere foyer, this one was quite something.

Max was playing the bland innocent to her reaction as he caught her arm and led her through one of the doors, but amusement twitched at his mouth.

'Ah—Mrs Walters.' A tall, thin woman with grizzled hair appeared in front of them. Max drew Clea towards her. 'You two will no doubt remember speaking to one another occasionally over the phone. Miss Maddon, Mrs Walters,' he introduced formally.

'It's nice to meet you at last, Mrs Walters.' Clea found a smile, and sent it to the other woman, who gave a poor quality one in return. She was busy taking in Clea's obvious condition, sharp eyes running over her in frank disapproval.'

'Dinner is almost ready, Mr Latham,' his housekeeper informed Max, with enough coolness to make clear her feelings. Then she was gone, disappearing back through the door by which she'd appeared, leaving Clea ruefully considering herself to be rebuffed.

'She's an angel,' Max excused drily. 'I don't know what I would do without her and Mr Walters.' He reached out to open a door, moving lithely inside. 'He janitors the building for me,' he threw over his shoulder. 'The other wing to this floor is split into two smaller flats. One for the Walters and one my mother uses when she comes up to town. What would you like to drink?' He had moved to a drinks cabinet before turning to search her out. 'Something long and . . . ' His voice trailed away, muffled by the mockery in his slow smile when he caught Clea's expression.

Good grief! was all she could think, as she hovered over the threshold of yet another shockingly extravagant room.

Bold blues and bright whites vied for dominance. Two huge bay windows lit the room with sunlight, draped in royal-blue velvet. The carpet was blue with splashes in red woven into the large symmetrical design. The red, she noted dazedly, had been used for a contrasting splash of colour in a similar way the yellow had been used in the foyer. White walls, white kid-leather settees, red and blue satin cushions scattered about. He had even had the audacity to bring green into the room in the shape of plants, huge resin-sheened, rubber-type plants that climbed up the walls in contained abundance.

'You—you've surprised me,' she mumbled when her gaze eventually clashed with his.

His smile was half a grimace. 'I don't see why,' he drawled, and let his gaze linger explicitly on her for a moment. 'I always did go for the exotic . . . It suits you,' he observed hoodedly, 'this room.'

Clea let out a short laugh. 'You think me—exotic?'

Max shook his dark head in wry disbelief. 'You're certainly not sparing on your impact.' His eyes held hers for a fraction of a second, telling her something she couldn't interpret. 'Come in and sit down,' he commanded mockingly. 'You're standing there as if you expect the room to attack you!'

She did as he bade, mainly because she was too stunned to do anything else. She sank into one of the couches, accepting a tall glass from him as he sat down beside her, his eyes narrowed on the beautiful décor of his lounge.

'You don't like it,' he observed after a moment.'

Clea blinked like an owl. 'Oh—no, that isn't true. It—it's a lovely apartment . . . '

'But?'

She let her eyes go on another brief foray of the room. 'It . . . it isn't very easy on the senses, is it?' she posed tentatively. Then she shook off her confusion and smiled at him, relaxing back into the squashy leather. 'It has "you" stamped all over it. Bold, bright and restless . . . how do you ever relax in such an atmosphere? Even you must find the occasional need to find relief from all the raw energy you run on. I can't see you finding it in here.'

Max looked about him, as if seeing his home through new eyes. 'It pleases me,' was his defence. 'I can't stand indecisiveness. Insipidity breeds insipidity. Feed your mind only blandness, and that is exactly what you'll get back in return.'

Curiouser and curiouser, Clea mused fancifully, this was yet another Max Latham she was seeing.

'I've never brought any of my—anyone else here,' he told her suddenly, studying his glass. 'Call it an idiosyncrasy of mine. I like to keep the mood here free from—unwanted influence.'

Was that a warning or just an explanation? 'Then why am I being made an exception to your rule?'

His head flicked around to catch the troubled look on her face. 'Because you *are* the exception,' he stated softly.

Clea held that steady gaze. 'Because of the baby?'

Max hesitated, then nodded gravely. 'If that reason helps you to accept me and my home, then, yes, because of the baby.'

'Dinner is ready, Mr Latham,' Mrs Walters interrupted them, bringing an inner sigh of relief to Clea, because the conversation had taken a distinct turn for the worse in her opinion. But Max looked annoyed.

'Right, Mrs Walters. Thank you.' He got up, turning to nod curtly at the housekeeper. 'You can leave as soon as you like now.'

A dismissal in anyone's books. The woman melted away without another word, leaving a much cooler atmosphere behind her.

'She doesn't like me,' Clea guessed wryly. 'She thinks I'm trying to foist someone else's child off on you.'

'Go and put her right, then,' Max suggested, helping her to her feet, as though it was just part of his normal routine to haul overweight females up from low-cushioned chairs.

Clea lifted a dark eyebrow at him. 'She wouldn't believe me if I did. Why don't *you* tell her?'

'And spoil her fun?' he teased, laughing and ducking as Clea aimed a blow at his chin.

The constantly shifting mood between them shifted once again, into a pleasant congeniality that seemed to expect Max's arm to rest across her shoulders as he guided her through to another room. Clea liked his arm there, she even found herself leaning into him, twisting her head back on to his shoulders so that she could smile up into his face.

'I hope you're not going to feed me boar's head stuffed with apples?' she joked when she saw the medieval décor of the dining-room.

Max let out a husky laugh. 'I don't think Mrs Walters's culinary skills will stretch that far!'

'More wine?' Max lifted the bottle from its bed of ice and waved it at her. Clea covered her glass with a hand, giggling at him.

'I think I've had enough,' she judged. 'See!' she went on to accuse him. 'I'm tiddly. It isn't done to get women in my condition drunk. Doesn't go with your image.' They were sitting quite close, using only a corner of the long, solid oak dining-table. They had shared the well cooked summer meal with a bottle of light white wine, but Clea was well aware that she had let him fill her glass more than he should have done. And abstinence over the last few months meant the wine had hit her system far quicker than it usually would do.

He raised mocking brows at her. 'What do you mean, "my image"?'

Clea picked up and sipped from the glass she had just covered up, purple eyes teasing him over the rim. 'You know! That macho sophistication you have that should have you running, rather than admitting to spending your free time with a pregnant woman.'

She was only teasing him, but Max didn't take it that way. His expression cooled, silver threads slashing into the smoky blue eyes. 'I've never denied you or our child to anyone!' he defended haughtily. 'It's *you* who denies *me* —surely?'

'That just isn't true!' She put down her glass to glare her protest at him.

'Then why haven't you done anything about my meeting your family?' he challenged coolly.

Clea shifted uncomfortably on her chair, lowering her gaze from his. 'I . . . I w-was going to mention it to them, when I go to stay with them for the weekend,' she mumbled.

'You spend most of your weekends with them?' Max enquired.

Clea nodded, a fond smile curving her generous mouth, fingers idling once again on her wine glass. 'They like to spoil me a little, and it pleases them to think they're giving me a break from London.'

'From being on your own, you mean,' he amended

grimly.

'Did you know my stepfather knows Joe?' she remembered suddenly.

Max revealed his surprise in a lift of an eyebrow. 'Have you seen Joe since you left me?'

An odd way of putting it. She sent him a searching glance, but Max was revealing very little. 'No.' She shook her head again, the glistening tresses of black hair whispering against her back, crackling with life. 'But I will be doing this weekend. Joe and his wife are coming to a party James and my mother are giving—on Saturday night. It will be nice to see him again', she sighed.

Max lifted a hand, almost absently reaching out to capture a lock of long black hair, and twisting it around his finger, his expression thoughtful. 'Let me take you to the party.'

Clea looked carefully at his implacable face that, as usual, told her nothing, though those blue eyes glittered with a strange intentness. 'I thought you said you preferred to meet my parents here, "on home ground", as you called it. Surely a large gathering isn't quite the place to make and gain accurate impressions?'

'Ashamed of me, Clea?' he taunted.

Her scalp was tingling, sending out warnings to the rest of her senses to beware, and she couldn't think straight for the slow burn of excitement beginning to run through her veins. She blamed the wine, and Max, because he was playing so delicately with her hair.

'Suspicious, more like,' she answered him honestly. 'I'm confused as to your motives.'

Max looked directly at her, capturing her gaze, and the warning tingles swept down her body.

'I thought I made my motives entirely clear yesterday,' he drawled, so quietly that Clea sensed a change in his mood, too. 'Marriage is my ultimate goal. If to achieve that I have to pass a barrage of tests from various sources, then, so be it.' He dropped her hair, and Clea choked back the groan of protest that leapt to her lips. Weak, Clea! She rebuked herself. This man is your worst weakness! 'Meeting and gaining the acceptance and respect of your parents is an important test,' he continued.

'You keep talking of marriage, as though it had become an essential solution to your continued existence!' she snapped, aware that her irritation had roots in an entirely different source than Max's constant reference to marriage.

His smile was full of whimsy, and entirely new to Clea. She found herself hooked on it instantly. It hinted at so much and gave nothing away.

'Can I escort you to the party?' he pushed with gentle insistence.

'No!' she refused, getting up quickly from the table. This whole situation was getting out of hand! Her body was telling her one thing, while her mind said another. Max was hinting at things she didn't dare consider, while that mocking tilt to his mouth denied them. She'd had too much wine, too much good company—and it was time to call a halt to the proceedings before she did something stupid and made a complete fool of herself! 'I'll speak to them about meeting you while I'm there this weekend. But I don't think it will be a good idea to launch you on to them with no warning . . . '

'There *are* such things as telephones,' he pointed out wearily as he, too, came to his feet, making a mockery of her weak excuse. 'And it is only Wednesday tomorrow . . .' Point made, he looked at her averted face for a moment, and the silence became tense. Then he sighed, and moved to stand beside her. 'Come on, I'll take you home. You look—tired.'

Clea moved beside him with the miserable feeling that she had disappointed him in some way. Of course, it

would be easy enough to call her mother and warn her that
Max would be coming with her. Just as it would be easy to
concede this one request to him without putting up her
usual stubborn protests.

What is happening to you? she wondered tiredly. Can't
you even meet him half-way? He's gone out of his way to
prove to you that he cares—has cared all along! Didn't
you acknowledge that yourself—didn't you actually stand
there and admit to yourself that you had been behaving
like a bitch towards him?

'I'm sorry,' she mumbled.

'What for?' he enquired coolly, holding open the
dining-room door for her.

She shrugged dully, unsure still—or unwilling—how to
say what she was thinking. He looked big, all of a sudden,
imperious with his dark face closed to her, that lean body
sending out a warmth her own remembered with bitter
yearning. Here stood the man she loved. Was it his fault
that he couldn't return her feelings? She went to pass
wearily by him, then stopped, turning to him, her hand
going out to lightly touch his arm, her eyes dark with an
unhappiness that cut into him.

'I'm sorry.' She tried again, swallowing on the lump of
weak emotion forming in her throat, determined this time
to admit her own pig-headedness and invite him to the
party. 'I'm sorry if I . . . '

Max swore thickly, cutting her small speech short as his
hands came up to grip her shoulders. 'For God's sake,' he
grated roughly, 'don't go humble on me, Clea! I don't
think I could stand it on top of everything else!' He stared
down at her, eyes glinting strangely, then he sighed heavily
and said, with diminishing patience, 'I don't want your
contrition! I don't want your meek resignation to my
presence in your life! I want more—much more!'

'I don't understand.' She was quivering in his grasp,

disturbed by the force of emotion he was using.

That inconsistent mood shifted yet again, tilting on to an upward spiral that began swirling frantically around them.

Her hand, quite without her being conscious of it, had slid up the silk covering on his arm, and across the width of his chest, to come to rest on the open V of his shirt, and her fingertips were quite absently stroking at the tangle of short dark hair curling there.

She went very still, shock at her own actions widening her eyes. Beneath her palm she could feel the thud of his heart, tripping oddly, then accelerating to a strong hammer. Tension sprung between them—strong sexual tension that made the sudden silence between them a dangerous substance. Max dragged in a deep breath, his chest moving fiercely beneath her hand—and she flinched, beginning to jerk away. Max stopped her, bringing up one of his hands to cover hers, holding it hard against his pounding breast.

'You shouldn't have done that,' he told her huskily. 'You shouldn't have touched me like that, Clea.'

He didn't need to elaborate. She knew exactly what he meant. Her touch had been an instinctive sensual caress, done as an unconscious cry from her inner self to that part of him she never ceased yearning for, re-opening doors that had been closed for months, doors that, on re-opening, set loose emotions neither of them could deny.

Her lips parted, the pink tip of her tongue flicking out to moisten her lips in a nervous gesture. Her eyes seemed locked on their clasped hands, her body intensely aware of his closeness, tingling to life so it caught at her breath and held her trapped.

'I . . . ' She tried to speak, to say something to break the fraught atmosphere, but her words died in her thickening throat.

Max muttered something, drawing her against him,

folding her into his arms. 'Look at me!' he demanded roughly.

She looked, and her body quivered at the blaze she encountered in his smoky-blue eyes. 'Max——' she breathed. 'You can't want . . . '

'Oh, I can,' he interrupted tensely, knowing exactly what she had been about to say. 'I've never stopped wanting!' he rasped. 'Can you honestly believe that because you're pregnant, swollen with our child, that I can't want you?' He laughed, a harsh, self-derisive, husky sound. 'Oh, I want,' he mocked. 'I want a lot of things!'

His mouth came down on hers with no warning. One moment he had been talking quickly and roughly, the next his mouth covered hers and he was dragging her as close to him as he could bring her, his lips forcing hers apart in a kiss that revealed a terrible hunger.

Clea swayed against him, overwhelmed by the sudden flare of desire between them. The kiss went on and on, weakening her with a need that fired her blood, matching the fire she knew raced through him.

Max groaned something unintelligible against her mouth, his arms tightening jerkily. 'I've needed this!' he rasped. '*Needed* this——'

His big body arched, curving her to him, the force of his kiss sending her head back against his supporting arm, and her senses swam away on a wild current of frantic desire. Clea clung shamelessly to him, fingers lost in the dark silkiness of his hair, nails scraping at his scalp, drawing groans of pleasure from him. Their mouths parted on a mutual need to throw themselves into a passion too long denied. Hands, bodies, senses, grappling with an embrace that was quickly whirling out of control, there in the doorway to his dining-room.

'Not here,' he choked as his hand closed over one full rounded breast, his thighs hard and pulsing against her swollen tummy, leaving Clea in no doubt as to how desperate his desire was. 'Let me love you, Clea,' he pleaded hoarsely. 'Please let me love you tonight.'

'Yes,' she whispered, unable to manage more than that soft, sensual encouragement.

His body shuddered on a release of tension, and he looked hotly down on her, smoky eyes consuming her love-flushed face. 'Just don't hate me for it later,' he muttered huskily. 'I don't think I could stand it if you hated me any more than you already do.'

Clea blinked, swimming up from the depths of sensuality long enough to frown at him in puzzlement. 'I don't hate you, Max,' she told him softly. 'I could never hate you.'

He searched her vulnerable face for a long tense moment, then sighed shakily, scooping her up in his arms and carrying her, her body gripped closely to him, to a darkened bedroom.

Clea could see nothing but Max as he placed her in the middle of the bed then dropped down beside her. He didn't speak, but his eyes were caressing as they ran over her face. Her hair was in wild array on his pillows, his hand very gentle as it stroked the soft skin of her shoulder.

'I've dreamed for months of seeing you here, Clea, on my bed, with me beside you.' His voice was like rough silk, sliding over the sensitised nerve-ends beneath her skin. 'I lie awake for hours, wondering what you look like with your body full of my child, swollen, firm. Have you any idea how erotic dreams like that can be?' he murmured. 'How could you think that I ever stopped wanting you? You're beautiful, beautiful . . . ' he repeated huskily, and covered her mouth once again.

His hand slid to her breast, covering the full mound, his thumb locating and gently caressing the throbbing nipple. Fire licked through her at frightening speed, making her arch in an attempt to escape the source, and she gasped.

'Max . . . ' she breathed in confused entreaty.

'Ssh,' he soothed, brushing his lips across hers. 'Don't think. You want this, Clea, as much as I do.'

It was true; she accepted it on a soft sigh that whispered across his face, and drew that mouth back to hers in a clinging kiss that sank them both into oblivion. Max wanted her, just as passionately as he used to do, and she couldn't fight that. She had always known it, and that was why she had erected all those hostile barriers against him, because she had known that to allow him close would end like this, with them losing themselves in one another.

Her hands lifted to his shoulders, stroking along the tensed muscles, revelling in the ripples of pleasure that shook him. Her fingers buried themselves in his hair, loving its silken texture, holding his mouth to hers. Their tongues touched, and she trembled on a shock of pleasure.

Max muttered something beneath his breath and jerked away from her, a dark flush streaking his cheekbones, fingers trembling as they fumbled with his clothes in his eagerness to free his body, to enjoy the aching sweetness of her touch. Then he was gently turning her so he could slide down the zip on her dress, helping the material to glide down her body with hands that trembled, eyes dark with hungry desire to look upon each part of her revealed to him until she, too, was naked and lying, locked by the intensity of his gaze as it ran over her.

On a soft sigh, he touched the tip of her breast with a single infinitely gentle finger. Her breasts were fuller than they used to be, the dark circles around the throbbing tip larger and much darker. The nipple, as he coaxed it into tingling life, was a long, tender nub that drew his mouth on to it in fascination.

With her hands locked behind his neck, Clea could only lie, lost in pleasure as he explored the new curves of her body with infinite care, his hands lingering on the firm mound where their child lay slumbering inside her womb. She felt no shame or embarrassment, only an incredible feeling of pride. His mouth ravished her breasts, moving urgently from one throbbing tip to another in rapid succession, arousing her with a heated gentleness that overwhelmed her. She reached out a hand to caress him in return, but Max firmly replaced it around his neck, refusing her desire to please him.

'Clea . . .' he whispered.

His heart slammed against her, his body racked with deep shudders of desire. Then they were caught in the wild rhythm of need, all conscious thought lost as they were hurled onwards, out into sensuous space, far beyond anything they had ever shared before.

CHAPTER ELEVEN

CLEA must have slept because, when she next became aware, the soft light of a summer dawn was threading through the window. She was in Max's arms, his hard body curled against the back of hers, his arms cocooning her to him. His hand splayed across her womb, their baby kneading softly against it, comforting her.

It was idyllic, this, she thought sadly. And dangerous, because it matched exactly so many of her secret yearnings. The soft, warm feel of his breath on her hair told her that Max was still sleeping. He was relaxed, his arm heavy on her, their bodies damp with sweat in the warmth of the room. Max must have covered them both, because a thin sheet was thrown over them. How long had he lain awake while she slept? she wondered. What had he been thinking?

Problems stirred to life, and she stirred with them, moving as stealthily as she could out of his arms, and sliding to the edge of the bed, scraping her hair back from her face with a hand before sitting to gather her thoughts, taking stock of where she was.

It could only be his bedroom. Max's character was stamped all over the deep tones of rusts, browns and black. Very masculine, she observed wryly, very Max.

Her dress lay in a heap on the floor beside the bed, and she bent to retrieve it, pulling herself into a standing position and arching slightly to ease the several aches in her body. She felt sluggish, languid after their loving.

'What are you doing?' His voice was slurred with sleep.

Clea turned her head to look at him. Max lay as she had left him, half covered by the sheet, his arms resting where her body had just been. He looked sleepy-eyed, and she smiled at him, because there was a look of the boy about him in this half-light.

'Getting dressed,' she said quietly, stepping into her dress and pulling it up over her body. She sat down on the bed, her back facing him. 'Fasten me up, would you?'

There was a pause, and Clea sensed a grimness in him, but didn't turn to confirm it. Then his fingers were deftly dealing with the zip, their touch impersonal.

'Where do we go from here?' he murmured once his hands had left her.

Good question, thought Clea. Where *do* we go from here? 'I don't know,' she answered honestly.

Max pulled himself up on the pillows, sombrely studying her profile. It had never been easy to read her, but just now her expression gave nothing away, other than an odd blankness.

'No backward steps this time, Clea,' he warned grimly.

She shook her head, agreeing with him. Her hair tumbled down her back to brush the mattress, eyes like violets, wide and startling, her hands resting absently on her swollen stomach. She looked the epitome of maternal woman, and his heart lurched with some answering masculine reply, making him want to gather her close again, but he dared not. He wasn't sure whether last night had been a mistake or not. The answer to that had yet to come out.

'I didn't plan seduction when I brought you here last night, you know.'

That brought her gaze around, on to him. 'I never for one moment thought you did,' she assured him. Max could be a swine, she knew that, but not that much of a swine.

Blue eyes held purple for a long moment. 'We both wanted it.'

'Yes,' she agreed quietly.

'Needed it.'

'Yes,' she agreed once again.

He folded his arms across his chest, watching her face carefully. 'And it's going to happen again. I won't just fade off the scene, because we've found we still have a—need for each other.' He was choosing his words with care, even Clea realised that. So he added softly, 'I need you again, right now.'

This time she nodded mutely in agreement, her expression solemn. Max sighed impatiently. 'Are you going to just sit there and agree with everything I say?' he mocked angrily. 'How am I supposed to know what you think if you don't tell me?'

'But I don't know what I think,' she answered quite levelly. It was the truth, she just didn't know! And it was that which was bothering her, this odd refusal to grapple with the problem. 'Take me home, Max,' she appealed suddenly. 'I can't think here, I can't seem to . . .'

Her hand lifted to her brow, rubbing at the frown marring it. Max reached out to grab her hand, moving it from her face so he could look worriedly at her. 'I didn't hurt you last night, did I?' He had gone pale at the thought. 'You're all right? I tried to be gentle, but I . . .'

'It was beautiful,' she assured him gently. She couldn't—wouldn't lie about that. 'You didn't hurt me. I'm just—confused, I think.' The frown came back. 'Will Mrs Walters mind if I make myself a drink?' She stood up, taking him by surprise and moving jerkily away from him.

'Of course she won't mind!' Max protested irritably. 'Clea, why don't you come back here?' He patted the space beside him in the big bed. 'We'll talk this thing through in comfort. There's no need for you to go back to your flat yet. You can . . .'

'I need a drink,' was her reply. And she was gone, gliding through the door before he had an opportunity to say any more.

Max joined her within minutes, dressed only in a dark robe, as though making a statement that he wasn't yet prepared to concede and take her home. Clea had made a pot of tea, and was sitting at the rich redwood table in the middle of his modern redwood kitchen. She poured them both a cup, and he pulled out a chair and sat down opposite her.

'We have to talk this through,' he insisted as soon as he sat down.

'Yes, I know. Max . . .' her voice drawled thoughtfully. She had been staring into her teacup, watching the steam curl up from the hot liquid, but now she lifted her eyes to his. 'Have I been behaving like a sanctimonious prig?'

His mouth took on an small upward curve. 'Did I say that?' he mused mockingly. Then he sighed, and there was more mockery in the soft sound. 'Yes,' he replied, and shrugged. 'Not that you didn't have a right to,' he added. 'If I can be a self-centred swine, why can't you be a little sanctimonious? We're none of us perfect.'

There was a message for her in there somewhere, but Clea refused to look for it. Instead, she sipped at her tea. 'I won't marry you,' she told him suddenly.

Max stiffened. 'Who asked you?' he came back curtly.

Clea smiled, because she knew he had been leading up to suggesting it. 'I must have counted at least four different women you've found comfort in over the past months.'

'Are you back to character assassinating, Clea?' he drawled. 'Since you refused any kind of relationship with me—legal or otherwise—I don't see that you have the right to comment on my private life.'

'True,' she conceded. Then added, curiously, 'But how

would you feel if, when this is all over—the baby, I mean—if I take another lover?'

His face tightened at that, eyes narrowing to cold slits. 'You're digressing somewhat.'

I'm trying to understand how you feel about me, she answered silently. His feelings towards her had certainly changed, she would have to be stupid not to realise that after last night Max had revealed a desperate need for her that went deeper than the mere physical. It reminded her of the rare times before the baby when he had become frantic in her arms; only, then, he'd hated the feeling it left him with, and now he was willing to face it openly.

'OK,' he sighed suddenly. 'You've made your point. I would hate to think of another man touching you. And that therefore means you have the right to feel the same about me. Do you,' he added curiously, 'hate to think of me with other women?'

I despise it, she thought, and smiled slowly. 'This is becoming very profound, isn't it? I tell you what . . .' She sat back in her chair to look directly at him, eyes wide and bland. 'I'll come and live with you. How does that appeal? I'll move in here for the time it will take for us both to wear out whatever it is that makes us want each other so badly.'

She was goading him into something, though he didn't know what. Max eyed her suspiciously, trying to peer through the bland mask she wore. 'And the baby?' he asked.

She shrugged. 'We wanted each other before, and we still want each other, despite the baby. If you're suggesting it's morally wrong, then I can't see the difference. Being your mistress with a child or without it makes no difference to the morality in the relationship.'

'I've never lived with a woman before,' he murmured absently.

'Have you ever wanted one as you want me, before?'

He thought about that quite seriously, then said, 'No, I want you quite desperately, Clea. I have to admit that. But what about you? What are you planning to get from such an unsatisfactory arrangement?'

'Who said it was unsatisfactory to me?' she challenged. 'I have to say at this point, Max,' she went on, throwing him an obstacle, 'I don't know for how much longer we can make love before the baby is born. I'll have to enquire.'

'You're talking about this as though it were just some cold business deal!' He was becoming angry with her. Clea stayed calm. Couldn't he hear himself? she thought wryly. Couldn't he make the comparison she was trying to draw for him, between himself when he'd commissioned her as his lover, and the way she was doing it now to him?

'OK,' he agreed suddenly, making her blink. He was eyeing her in a calculating way that made her stir uncomfortably. 'You can move in with me. Right away. Today,' he announced firmly, standing up and moving around the table towards her. 'We'll close up your flat for the time being—until you're ready to break this off between us. Then it will still be there, waiting for you to return to when the time comes. Now let's go back to bed.' He grasped her arm, pulling her, bewildered, from the chair. 'We've got a couple of hours left before we need get up for real.'

'B-but . . .' she stammered helplessly. This wasn't going the way she'd expected it to. Max had thrown her by agreeing to her proposition. She'd expected him to turn tail and run!

'No buts,' he commanded. 'I'm tired, even if you're not. We can discuss details later.'

'But, Mrs Walters . . .'

A dark brow rose sardonically. 'She'll have to get used

to finding you in my bed some time. Why not now?' he pointed out quite logically, his hand firm on her arm as he took her back into the bedroom. 'I see no sense in forsaking a warm and comfortable bed for the sake of the misplaced sensibilities of my housekeeper.'

It wasn't her sensibilities I was thinking of, Clea thought mulishly, as he turned her around and deftly dealt with the zip on her dress, so it was once again falling into a heap on the floor.

She didn't see the amused tilt to Max's mouth. She had no idea how he was aware that he had just called her bluff and turned it to his own advantage. 'Mmm,' he murmured, placing his lips to her shoulder. 'Like silk.' His hands curved her thickened waist, pulling her back against him, face buried in the soft fall of her beautiful hair. 'Delicious. My warm and sensual Clea. Wild and wanton Clea . . . I could lose myself in your sweetness . . .'

'Max . . .' She was trembling with the emotions he stirred in her, her mind beginning to swirl.

'I know.' He sighed tragically. 'It's late, and you're too tired. So am I, come to that—let's go to bed.'

That wasn't quite what she'd meant when she had uttered his name in that husky way, but Clea didn't correct him, sighing contentedly as she coiled up against him beneath the thin sheet.

I've done it again, she acknowledged as she slipped into sleep, I've let him take me over again. Weak, Clea, she rebuked herself, but couldn't find any strength to go with the censure. Weak . . .

They slept, curled up in each other's arms, problems shelved until the morning proper. But the morning brought a whole new set of problems with it. Worries that managed to banish all the rest by the sheer weight of concern.

Max woke her with a kiss on her flushed cheek. 'Wake

up, sleepy head,' he murmured softly, his smiling face so
gentle, as it leaned over her, that it took a moment to
convince herself that she wasn't dreaming. 'I would much
rather have left you to sleep on,' he continued while she
struggled to throw off the mists of sleep. 'But I didn't
think you'd take kindly to my leaving you to face the
dreaded Mrs Walters on your own.'

He was already dressed for work in a dove-grey business
suit. His skin smelled of soap and felt smooth against her
cheek, his black hair was still damp from a recent shower,
his eyes were warm on her sleepy face.

'What time is it?' she mumbled, instinctively reaching
up to hook a lazy arm around his neck, bringing his face
closer to hers. 'Mmm, you smell nice—fresh and clean.'
She kissed him on the mouth, the embrace meandering
into a sluggish desire.

It was Max who pulled away, reluctance in the slowness
with which he disentangled himself. 'Don't tempt me,' he
sighed. 'It would be so easy to climb back in there with you
and forget everything else, but I daren't. Not if I'm going
to pack two days' work into one morning.'

He grinned at her puzzled expression. 'We're going to
move you in here, or have you forgotten? I thought I'd
pick you up here at lunch time, and we'd go over to your
flat to pack your things.'

'You don't mean to waste any time, do you?' she noted
wryly. 'What if I've changed my mind?'

Max shook his head. 'No can do,' he stated glibly. 'Now
you've had your wicked way with me, you're going to have
to stand by me.'

It was nice, all this. He *looked* like the 'day-time Max'
she was used to seeing at this time of the day, but in every
other way he was different: indulgent, tender—loving,
almost.

Clea smiled, and it was a slow, sensual smile that darkened her eyes and lent temptation to her soft mouth. 'It seems I've been trapped,' she sighed in mockery, privately amazed at the ease at which they were teasing each other about something that had rather sensitive undercurrents. 'But no lunch,' she refused sadly. 'I have to work till five. The packing will have to wait until then.'

Max sat away from her, swapping indulgence for gravity. 'Let me call Brad Gattings and tell him you won't be going in again,' he suggested huskily. 'I'll lend him one of my own secretaries until his own gets back, if it will ease your conscience. But don't go back there, Clea, please.'

She levered herself up on to an arm, using her free hand to push the tumble of hair from her face, revealing the stubborn set of her mouth. 'Don't spoil it, Max,' she advised softly, but with enough warning to carry.

He stood up abruptly. 'Have I any choice?'

But half an hour later they had to acknowledge that the choice had been taken away from both of them. Clea got up, showered, dressed in her white dress and made for the kitchen, praying that Mrs Walters hadn't yet arrived. She could do without the woman's disapproving stares this early in the morning.

Max was alone in the kitchen, to her relief. He had made a pot of coffee and, as she slipped into a chair at the kitchen table, he placed a round of freshly made toast in front of her. 'Eat,' he commanded, and Clea hid her amusement.

The old Max wouldn't have thought of making her coffee and toast! That one would have been out of the door as soon as he could make his get-away, off into that other world he occupied, lover forgotten for his real love—his company and the exhilarating challenges waiting for him there.

She sipped slowly at her coffee, aware of a nagging ache in her head, and a strange feeling of malady about her body; nothing to put her finger on, just a general sluggishness and the headache. Overtiredness, she put it down to, and a disturbed night, she thought wryly. She wasn't used to them any more, disturbed nights.

'I'll drive you home when you're ready,' Max offered, leaning against a shiny worktop to drink his coffee. He was eager to be off, yet containing it, prepared to wait.

In reward for his unusual thoughtfulness, Clea turned to smile at him. 'If you need to be off, I can always order a taxi. It *is* getting late, and I remember how you like to be in the office for eight-thirty.'

'I'll wait for you,' was his quiet, firm reply.

Clea accepted his word with no demur. Her head had begun to pulse rather alarmingly, and she stared distastefully at the coffee left in her cup. I feel decidedly ill, she thought dully. She hadn't suffered morning sickness for months, yet the feeling overwhelming her now was warning just that. She got up, swaying slightly when her legs wobbled beneath her. Her hand went unconsciously to her brow. A surge of heat prickled along her skin and she took in a deep gulp of air.

'I feel—strange,' she murmured to the watchful man close to her.

It seemed as if every pulse in her body had decided to make itself felt, thumping heavily, throbbing in a strange, frightening way, slow and sluggish, yet making her feel breathless, as though she'd been running. A desperate panic hit her from nowhere, setting up a mad buzzing in her ears, and she screwed up her face on a wave of pain.

'My head,' she moaned, pressing a hand to her brow, stumbling slightly as she tried to move. 'Max!'

A pleading hand went out towards him and was caught in a firm grasp. Max was reaching for her as she began to fall, her legs buckling beneath her. The whole episode could only have spanned mere seconds, yet she felt everything in strange slow motion. Her head pounded at the temples, and she knew at that precise moment that she was about to pass out.

Max caught her as she went, cursing softly as he scooped her up into his arms, his body muscles clenching to take the sudden extra weight.

'Damn you, Clea!' he rasped, and went pale when he looked took in the hectic flush on her face, felt the heat emanating from her body, and the way her pulses raced frighteningly. 'Damn your stubbornness!'

Dr Fielding arrived just as Clea showed signs of coming around, but she was dazed and not entirely aware of what was going on around her.

Max watched worriedly as the doctor examined her, took her blood pressure, listened for a long time to the baby's heartbeat. She had gone from burning hot to icy cold in moments. It had made Max frantic, because he didn't know what to do. Now she lay very still, her hand resting loosely in his, eyes closed and breathing shallow.

'I'll give her something to make her rest properly,' the doctor announced as a concluding mutter to his unrushed examination.

'No, I don't want anything.' Clea roused herself enough to refuse. 'No drugs, they're not good for the baby.'

Dr Fielding looked down on her pale face and raised bushy brows in a sardonic expression Clea missed because her eyes were still closed. 'And you think I would prescribe something that was *bad* for the baby?' he challenged haughtily. 'A mild sedative, nothing more, Miss Maddon,' he assured in his gentlest doctor's voice. 'Your blood pressure is way up. The only way to get it down is by complete rest—and I mean flat-on-your back, not-moving-off-the-bed kind of rest,' he added sternly, then turned his attention to Max.

'I should inform her mother,' he said frowningly. 'She

mustn't be on her own . . .'

'She's staying here,' Max stated grimly.

The doctor's eyes widened in surprise. 'But Miss Maddon is . . .'

'Having my baby,' Max put in harshly. His grip on her limp hand increased. 'You can be sure I'll take good care of her.' He dragged in a deep breath, trying desperately to grasp at control, his gaze locked on Clea's white face. 'I'm responsible for her. She's mine.'

'I was thinking of a few days in hospital, actually,' the doctor said gently.

'No hospital,' Max once again stated. 'Clea has a dislike for hospitals. Her father was confined to one for a long time before he died. She'll hate it there.'

The doctor hesitated assessingly, noting the strength of character, the set of Max's square jaw—and the way his gaze had hardly left the wan face on the pillows. Then he nodded mutely, and indicated that they should leave the room.

Having to force himself, Max stood up and followed the doctor from the bedroom. 'What's the matter with her?' he demanded as soon as they were out of earshot of Clea. He had spent the last thirty minutes torturing himself with the idea that he was directly to blame for Clea's unexpected collapse. If he hadn't . . .

'Overwork, overtiredness, high blood pressure—I could go on and blame the weather, plus a whole lot of other things, but I won't. I'll just say that I've been warning her for weeks now to ease up. Now her body has told her the same thing, but with more authority than I could manage.' He smiled wryly at that, as though Clea's stubbornness had already tested him greatly. 'She'll want her iron tablets. Perhaps you can get her to take them regularly! God knows, she's the worst pill-taker I've ever come across.'

'Yes,' said Max quietly. 'I know.'

Dr Fielding left, promising to call again in the morning. Max went back to the bedroom, to find Clea lying with her eyes open. 'How are you feeling?' he asked softly, coming to sit back on the bed beside her.

'Strange.' Her mouth twisted in self-mockery, face pale against the rich tan of the sheets. 'Did I frighten you?' she asked in a contrite whisper, noting his strained features. 'I'm sorry. I . . .'

He shut her up by the simple process of covering her mouth with a gentle finger. 'Don't you dare apologise to me,' he commanded. 'Not when this is all my fault! If I hadn't lost control and made love to you, if I had only shown a little bit of . . .'

Clea shook her head beneath the resting finger, and touched a kiss to the soft, warm pad, eyes dark with sympathy as they looked into his tormented ones.

'No one's fault but my own,' she stated softly. 'I've known for weeks that I should have been resting more. Our making love had nothing to do with it—unless you allow for a rather wicked desire to do it again!'

She was teasing him out of the doldrums. Clea could no more make love at this moment than she could raise her head off the pillow. She was weak, drained of every last bit of energy.

'Did Dr Fielding mention the baby?' she asked after a moment, her thready tone revealing how little she had wanted to ask that question, because she feared so much the answer.

Max put a light hand on her stomach, smiling reassuringly at her. 'The baby is fine. It's you we're worried about. You have to stay in bed and sleep. I have some mild sedatives to give you in a moment, when I've made you a warm drink. Then I've been ordered to stand guard over you and not let you even blink without permission!'

'I have to call my mother.' Her brow clouded, tiredness pulling at her eyelids, a natural worry for what her mother was going to do when she found out that she was ill taking what little colour she had from her face.

'I'll speak to your mother, Clea,' he assured her gently. 'And Brad . . .'

His hand came to cup her cheek, caring, his eyes smoky, unable to hide his concern. 'I'll see to everything. You just rest, hmm?'

Clea nodded mutely. She hadn't the strength or the desire to argue. Let Max deal with Amy, let him deal with Brad and everything else. It was good just to offload all those petty problems on to his shoulders and leave hers feeling pleasantly light for a change.

Her eyelids grew heavy, her body curling on to its side, lips blindly searching out and kissing that comforting hand. 'Poor Max,' she murmured. 'His gypsy has turned out to be a whole lot of trouble for him . . .'

'Not to me,' he denied softly. 'She has never been any trouble to me. You've done your utmost, Clea, to make it easy for me to walk away from you. The only thing you didn't take into account, was whether I *wanted* to walk away.'

'You wanted to before you knew about the baby,' she pointed out sleepily. 'A baby is no reason to hold on to a man who wishes to be let go—not in this day and age.'

They were talking softly, murmuring in the peacefulness of the room. Max looking grave. He had no adequate answer to give her, so he offered none. 'Get some sleep,' he said instead. 'I'll send in Mrs Walters with that drink and sedative.'

'Max . . .?' He had reached the door when she called him back. He turned to face her. Her eyes were open again, their liquid purple plucking at his heart. 'Thank you.'

'For what?' he enquired.

'For just being here, when I know you must have a thousand and one other things you should be doing.'

'Nothing is more important to me than you are—remember that,' he stated huskily. 'It means a lot to me that you believe it.'

Her eyes were already closing again, and he couldn't be absolutely sure that she'd heard him. He walked slowly towards the study, brow furrowing as his mind worked on his steadily mounting problems.

Max tapped restless fingers on the desktop as he waited for the telephone to answer. This, he knew, was not going to be easy. A deep, cool voice cracked down the line at him, and he sat up straight in his chair.

'James Laverne?' he enquired.

'Speaking,' came the cool reply.

'You may know my name——' Max began his grim task '—Max Latham. I'm calling about Clea . . .'

CHAPTER TWELVE

CLEA awoke to the wonderful feel of a soft breeze cooling her heated skin. The room was filled with sunlight filtering through the net curtains at the open window. It must be late, she thought, because it *felt* late. She let her gaze wander about her surroundings, taking longer than she should to recall where she was.

The sound of rustling paper brought her head swinging around to look over the other side of the room. Max sat in a cushioned chair, slumped over some papers on his lap, frowing in concentration. All around him were sheaves of papers, stacked on any available surface within reach of him, covering the ebony wood dressing-table, the tallboy, the floor around his feet. He had changed out of his business suit into casual trousers and a short-sleeved shirt in pale blue, showing off his tanned and muscled arms.

He appeared to have been there for quite a while. Perhaps he hadn't gone into work at all today, perhaps he had wanted to stay here with her . . .

She must have moved, because his head came up and around, blue eyes honing in on her face and lightening into a smile the moment he saw she was awake. She smiled shyly at him, and he stood up, dropping the rest of his papers to the floor before coming over to seat himself beside her on the bed.

'Hi,' he said softly, looking at her in a way that made her heart shift.

'Hi,' she returned, feeling distinctly at a disadvantage lying here, in his bed. 'Have I been asleep a long time?'

'Oh——' He glanced at his watch. 'About five hours, give or take a minute or two.' The smile came back, brief but warm. 'Thirsty?'

She nodded.

'I'll get Mrs Walters to make you something. What would you prefer, tea—coffee—something long and cool?'

'Cool, please,' she said, labouring to pull herself up against the pillows. Max was leaning over her in an instant, taking her by the shoulders and gently assisting her. It was only as she flopped weakly back against the pillows that she realised she was wearing one of her own nightdresses. She glanced at Max in surprise.

He grinned. 'Your mother's doing,' he informed her. Clea's eyes widened. 'She and your stepfather arrived barely an hour after I called them. Once she'd convinced herself that you were in good hands . . .' His mouth went awry when he said that, as though the moment of meeting Amy was a memorable one. '. . . She bustled off to your flat to pack the essentials for you. You were still dead to the world when she got back, so she banished James and me to the lounge and commandeered Mrs Walters to help make you more comfortable. You slept through it all like a baby,' he teased while Clea looked aghast.

'How did she manage to get over Mrs Walters's aversion to me?' The housekeeper had brought Clea's drink that morning after the doctor had left, but her manner had not warmed at all.

'Charm.' He laughed. 'And a blind refusal to believe that anyone could disapprove of her beautiful daughter. How in heaven's name could you have a mother like that, Clea?' He sounded bemused. 'I nearly fainted when she walked in here!'

'Ask James to tell you the story of his first meeting with me,' she suggested by way of a reply. 'He still hasn't quite recovered from the shock. Where is my mother now?'

'Back in her own home by now,' Max told her. 'James and I convinced her that you would be fine with me here to look after you. And I promised that, all being well with you, and if the doctor says it's OK, I'll bring you to her party on Saturday.'

'You have all been busy, haven't you?' she remarked a trifle mulishly, feeling oddly nettled by his easy disarming of her mother. 'Give you five minutes and you'd charm Methusela himself into liking you!'

'Thank you for that vote of confidence in my powers of persuasion,' he replied blandly, refusing to take the bait, but getting up as though removing himself from a potentially dangerous substance. 'I'll go and see about that drink.'

The next time she woke, it was dark outside, and she desperately needed to use the bathroom. Her head swam sickeningly as she levered herself into a sitting position. There was no light on in the room, and it felt strange—alien to her groggy senses. She was hot and sticky, her hair clinging limply to her because she had slept so long on it left loose.

She wished she was back in her own flat. At least there she could move about without disturbing anyone. What time was it, anyway? It could be the middle of the night for all she knew. Her head still throbbed and her body felt heavy. When she attempted standing up, she found her legs refusing to support her.

'Damn!' she muttered, sitting back down again.

'What is it?' The sharp enquiry made her jump, and she glanced up to find Max standing in the open doorway, light flooding in from the hall, revealing the thin black robe that was all he seemed to be wearing.

'I need to use the bathroom,' she muttered petulantly. This is great! she thought. Having to stoop to requesting assistance just to go to the toilet!

Max came to stand in front of her, and Clea lifted her arms in mute and glum compliance. He bent, sliding an arm beneath her knees and another beneath her shoulders. Clea wrapped her arms around his neck and he lifted her easily against him. Her head flopped on to his shoulder, and he sighed, as though sensing her frustration, but refraining from saying a word as he carried her into the bathroom that adjoined the bedroom.

'Be OK?' he murmured as he lowered her on to a padded bath stool.

She nodded, feeling miserable. Her shoulders lifted and fell on a long and soulful sigh. Max watched it happen, and after a small hesitation came to squat beside her, pushing the damp tangle of hair away from her face, and cupping her chin to make her look at him.

'How about a nice refreshing bath?' he suggested.

Clea nodded dully. She felt like a small, sickly child. And Max reminded her of her father: he used to coddle her like this when she was ill. Her mother had nursed her, but her father had given the necessary cosseting she had always seemed to need at times like these.

Tears, big globular ones, slipped from her unhappy eyes and ran down her cheeks. 'I h-hate this,' she choked.

'I know,' Max soothed huskily. His lips came to gently kiss away the tears, his breath warm and comforting on her face. 'Why don't I start the bath running, then leave you your privacy while I make a nice cold drink? Then we'll bathe you like a baby and put you back to bed, hmm?'

His eyes twinkled at her, appealing with her to find her sense of humour. Clea searched for a smile, and found it not far away. 'Useless creature,' she mocked herself.

'Absolutely useless,' he agreed with a smile.

The bath was a delight. And, true to his word, Max

bathed her while she lay there like some pampered princess, surrendering to his ministrations with no embarrassment. 'I could hire you out,' she mused, 'as a ladies' maid. I'd make a fortune!'

'Sorry,' he refused. 'I'm not for hire.'

He was kneeling by the sunken bath, having to bend double to cream the scented soap into her body. 'Shame,' she sighed, with a licking of her lips that was a deliberate provocation. 'You're rather good at this. It's rather erotic, having a man bathe you.'

'Don't put ideas into my head,' he warned on a wicked leer.

'You could join me, of course . . . save you having to bend over like that. And the bath is easily big enough to take us both.'

Her glinting gaze challenged him, and Max went still, staring at her in something close to horror. 'Are you suggesting what I think you're suggesting?'

Her eyes opened in wide-eyed innocence. 'I'm only trying to make the job easier for you!' She defended herself guilelessly.

'You're trying to seduce me!' he accused. 'And I'm afraid I won't be seduced, not until you're well again. Doctor's orders,' he told her smugly.

'Is that why you aren't sleeping in the same bed as me?'

'No,' he instantly denied. 'I just didn't want to disturb you. Hands up,' he commanded. 'We'll get you to your feet before I find a towel. I can control my baser instincts when I have to, you know,' he continued casually once they had her on her feet and dripping into the bath water while he went to fetch a huge fluffy towel. 'I can even sleep quite contentedly beside you without resorting to rape.' His brows twitched in wicked mockery. 'But it's too hot, and you would find it just too uncomfortable having someone beside you while you tried to rest.'

'Who said?' she challenged indignantly.

Max looked gravely down into her deep purple eyes, and saw the mute appeal lurking there. His hands stilled on the towel he was just wrapping around her, and something palpable settled between them. He dropped his gaze from hers and went back to rubbing her dry. But he didn't speak, and neither did Clea. It had all been said in that look.

When she was settled back in bed, feeling fresh again and with her hair brushed and neatly braided, Max handed her a tall glass of freshly squeezed and chilled orange juice, then disappeared for the moment it took him to settle the apartment back down for the night. Then he was back, sliding into the bed beside her, removing the glass, and switching off the bedside light before gathering her to him.

That was it, nothing said, but he never again chose a lonely bed in preference to sharing hers.

Thursday brought with it yet more hot weather, and a definite improvement in Clea's health. Dr Fielding was quietly satisfied with her progress, and saw no reason why she couldn't attend her mother's party on Saturday, so long as she didn't spend the evening 'kicking up hell' as he drolly put it. 'And on condition that you stay where you are for the rest of today and tomorrow,' he added with a look that brooked no argument, while Clea scowled her agreement.

Max went into the office for a few hours, leaving Clea to the dubious care of a still cool Mrs Walters.

When, in a third interruption of the book she was reading, Mrs Walters came into the room to put away freshly laundered clothing into the huge mirrored ebony wood wardrobes that lined one wall of the bedroom, her face stiff and discouraging, Clea lost her temper.

'Has Mr Latham informed you, Mrs Walters, that I shall be a permanent fixture here from now on?'

He hadn't. The other woman's severely stiffening form told Clea that. Damn you, Max! she raged silently. He could easily have dealt with this.

'Then I suggest you go away and think about it,' Clea went on in a tone those who knew her well would step back from. Clea, in cutting mood, was daunting. 'And, while you're considering whether you want to continue working here under *my* instruction, I suggest you also consider the fact that, come October, there will be a baby to add to your—workload.' Clea declined the opportunity to throw the woman's rude attitude back in her face; she could see quite well that Mrs Walters was clear on what was really being said. 'Of course, we will understand if you decide the changes to come here will be too much for you.'

She eyed the housekeeper speculatively, curious as to why she had been treated to a cold shoulder since she'd come here. Surely the woman wasn't so old-fashioned?

Mrs Walters turned, as if to leave the room, then paused and turned back to face Clea. 'Mr Latham has never brought one of his—women here before,' she informed Clea coldly. 'He's naturally kind to those in trouble, and easily put upon because of it.'

And there, thought Clea, is the crux of the matter.

'This baby I'm carrying is his,' she put in gently.

The disapproval didn't diminish. 'I know, he told me.' Thank you, Max. At least he had tried. 'But he hasn't married you, has he?'

Clea took up the challenge. 'Because I refused to marry him,' she informed the cold-faced woman. 'And that,' she went on curtly, 'is all the explanation you're getting, Mrs Walters. So think over what I've said, will you?' And with that, Clea returned to her book, the dismissal as good as any Max could dish out, but then, she had been taught by the master himself.

Next time Mrs Walters entered the bedroom, there was a

distinct change in attitude. What had caused it, Clea could
only guess at, but she accepted its fragile terms with no
comment, and simply softened her own manner to suit.

Friday brought yet another surprise. Clea was just
considering getting up and taking a nice long shower. Max
was at work, Mrs Walters out shopping, the apartment
was very quiet, and she was bored—when she heard the
front door open and close, listened frowningly to the tread
of a stranger's feet coming down the hallway, opening
doors and closing them again, as though the intruder was
checking each room for occupants. Then her bedroom
door swung open and Clea blinked, the fear that had
begun clamouring inside her as those feet grew closer,
dying, to be replaced with a different emotion. One of
defensive surprise.

'You must be Clea,' said a well modulated, if brisk
voice.

Good grief! thought Clea. The cavalry has arrived!

Tall and statuesque, her intruder stood like a sergeant
major, one capable hand grasping the doorknob, the other
clamped tightly to her side, black patent handbag hanging
from a clenched fist that looked like it could pack quite a
punch if necessary.

If it hadn't been for those clear blue eyes and sleek
arched brows on features hewn from rock, Clea would
have been yelling for help by now. The new arrival moved,
marching over to stand by the bed, magnificent silvered
hair swirled into a sleek topknot on that elegant head, suit
of navy twill sadly bare of any military gold trim. Those
piercing eyes fixed themselves on Clea's bemused face.

'You shouldn't be surprised,' remarked Mrs Latham.
'My son had to acquire his arrogance from somewhere.
It's all in the genes.'

Clea couldn't help it, she laughed, and the blue eyes
twinkled, a broad smile softening that craggy face.

The handbag was discarded carelessly, and Max's mother pulled up a chair and sat down without invitation.

'So, you think my son's not fit husband material.'
Good grief.

'I don't blame you,' continued that quick, no-nonsense voice. 'He's an out and out rake! Utterly disreputable. I tried disowning him once, but he wouldn't listen to me. You know how that feels, don't you?' Those shrewd eyes read Clea's mind as if it were an open book. 'Has a terrible will of his own, my son,' she stated bluntly. 'Likes everything to run in straight lines—no undulations . . .' Her hand flapped out to draw huge waves in between them. 'That's why he so good with computers. They suit his character. You do, too.'

'Oh, but . . .' Clea went to protest, but was shut off by a firm shake of a silvered head.

'That other side to his nature, you do,' affirmed Max's mother, as though she knew Clea inside out. 'That dark, wild side he likes to keep hidden. Why won't you marry him. It *is* his child, is it not?'

Clea nodded her head in reply to the last question, swallowed—in evasion of the first, and blinked in an effort to pull herself together before Max's mother trampled all over her!

'We—we weren't expecting you.' She managed to gather together a whole sentence.

'Max was,' informed his mother. 'That's why he's conspicuous in his absence. Max and I strike sparks off one another. He doesn't like to admit that I have more common sense than he does; he doesn't like me bullying him because he thinks I have an unfair advantage over him, being a frail old lady now . . .'

Frail! Hah! thought Clea. There is nothing even

vaguely frail about this woman.

'Which is why that woman who looks after him isn't around, either,' Clea was informed candidly. 'I scare her to death . . . Do I scare you?' An eyebrow rose questioningly, giving Clea need to smother a giggle.

'No,' she answered with only the slightest quiver to her smiling lips. 'You're just like Max—all bark, no bite.'

'Good.' Mrs Latham seemed satisfied with Clea's reply, because she settled herself more comfortably on the chair, and the bold manner fell away to be replaced with a surprisingly homely one. 'Now, tell me all about it. Begin at the beginning and don't stop until you reach the other end. Then I'll make my own conclusions and let you know who I think is being the bigger fool.'

'And which of us received the wooden spoon?' Max enquired with faked bated breath.

They were curled up in bed after a bewildering evening of his mother's wayward company. Clea, who had been allowed to get up for dinner, had sat listening to the Latham by-play in growing amazement, as Mrs Latham chipped chunks off Max's patience with a sharp and lethal appraisal of his faults, while he just sat there and took it! It came as a revelation to Clea to compare the way he took his mother's censure with the way he had treated her during the last months when she had aimed her bitter darts at his grim head. He wasn't known for his forbearance. Yet with her now and, as she now knew, his mother, he was prepared to put up with any amount of provocation before showing a healthy retaliation.

By the time his mother retired to her own flat, they were both sighing with relief. 'Now you know why she has her own flat to go to,' Max said wryly as they made ready for bed. 'She can run rings around me, and I don't consider myself easy play.'

'Why is that, do you think?' Clea quietly enquired, pausing as she braided her hair, feeling the breathlessness of nervous anticipation hold her. His reply was that important to her.

He shrugged, unaware of her stillness. 'Because I love her, I suppose,' he murmured ruefully. 'To cut her down—as I know I could do—would hurt her, and I would never want to do that. It's easier to let her think she has me under her thumb.' He turned to flash a wide grin at Clea. 'She knows she can only go so far, though, before I put the brakes on her.'

Like me, thought Clea on a tremor of staggering discovery. Like me!

'Oh, I was judged the bigger fool,' Clea admitted as they cuddled together in the darkness. 'She said that if I'd had just an ounce of sense I would have married you like a shot, then ruthlessly bled you of every penny I could get before divorcing you again.'

'So much for mother love,' Max murmured, but absently. He had become engrossed in tasting her earlobe, sucking it into his mouth and biting sensuously on the sensitive flesh. 'I call that a plotting of my destruction . . . Clea . . .' he groaned. 'Do you think . . .?'

His voice became husky, a rasping incitement to her racing pulses, and she found she had no defence against it. Turning in his arms, she reached up to kiss the shallow cleft in his chin, lush black lashes sliding upwards to reveal eyes dark purple with desire.

'You're the man with all the answers,' she whispered. 'Do *you* think . . .?'

Clea awoke the next morning with a feeling of wellbeing that reached right down to her toes. She was up and dressed before Max had even come up for air, her soft, slightly husky voice meandering its way into his dreams as she moved about the apartment, humming to herself.

'You sound happy.' He caught up with her in one of the guest bedrooms, where she was eyeing the stark décor with the look of one preparing an attack.

She turned to smile at him, her hair flowing free and glistening down her back, her dress a pretty lemon-print strappy smock that left her shoulders and throat bare.

'I am,' she told him. 'Very.'

Their eyes held for a long moment, exchanging messages their minds wouldn't allow them to voice. Then Clea turned back to her study of the room, cutting the connection. 'I think this room would make a nice nursery,' she mused.

'Ah,' he said. 'Now I understand that calculating look. You're going to take my mother's advice, and begin spending my money.'

Her answering grin was pure mischief. 'When in doubt, consult the expert!'

He looked the boy again, with his hair all ruffled and eyes heavy with recent sleep. He was leaning negligently against the open doorway, hands shoved into deep robe pockets. So different from how he had looked last night, lost to passion: all man then, hard, sure, sensual man. Her heart twisted painfully because she was aware of how vulnerable she was allowing herself to become, how easy it was to convince herself that he cared for her more deeply than he would admit. A dangerous path to tread, but one she could no longer deny herself.

In just a few short days he had made himself indispensable to her. She blamed it on her condition, and could only hope that, once the baby was born, and her emotions had returned to normal, she would then find the strength to walk away with dignity.

'Come here,' he demanded softly, lifting an inviting

hand towards her. 'I need my morning fix.'

The kiss was warm and long and tender, his arms a haven, into which she willingly walked.

CHAPTER THIRTEEN

AMY'S party was more a barbecue, professionally taken care of by hired caterers who had set up in a corner of the garden near the house. The garden had been hung with pretty, coloured lanterns. Tables and chairs were dotted about the wide patio, with white linen tablecloths and brightly coloured napkins. The whole effect was one of a lovely English summer party. Music played softly through the rooms in the house, piped throughout by some central hi-fi system. A four-piece band played dance music in the drawing-room, the big french windows were thrown wide to welcome the evening air.

Clea moved from group to group, with Max's arm possessive about her slender shoulders, her blood-red silk caftan a perfect foil to her dark beauty. Her hair tumbled in glittering waves, wild and free as Max liked it, drawn away from her face with a large red comb studded with flashing rhinestones.

She introduced Max, they chatted lightly, and all curiosity was left unquenched, because no one would be ill mannered enough to ask outright if Clea's obvious condition was due directly to the man beside her, and neither Clea nor Max were giving out that kind of information.

Some knew Max already, others had only heard of him through their business interests in the City. Most were instantly impressed with his easy sophistication, and his male attraction did not go unnoticed by the female members of the party. But then, neither did the beauty Clea radiated as she rested easily in the arc of her man's arm.

'You should have brought your mother,' Amy scolded when she heard Max's mother was in town. 'What must she think of us—leaving her on her own in London while we make merry?'

Max shook his dark head. 'She couldn't make it,' he said. 'She has a tendency to plan out every available minute of her London excursions with a military precision.' Clea giggled, and Max turned laughing eyes on her to share the private joke—she had told him what her first fanciful impression of his mother had been. Max had been highly amused. 'Tonight she's booked out to a group of old friends, from the days when she lived in town. She sends her apologies and her regards, and asked me to invite you all down to Devon once the baby producing is over.'

Amy flushed with pleasure. 'Oh, how kind of her!'

They wandered the spacious rooms, their relaxed journey taking them outside and in, and Clea noted with a deep inner pride that Max was by far the most attractive man present tonight, semi-formally dressed in black silk trousers that hugged the long length of his powerful legs, and an oyster-pink shirt left casually open at the throat.

Two exclusive people, whose mutual contentment with life filled the air space around them. His gentle attentiveness to Clea was a statement of possession in itself, and her contentment within it a pleasure to witness.

They found Joe and his wife, Cassie, and spent a long time talking, Clea fielding Joe's frankly enquiring gaze with a blandness that refused to appease his curiosity. Max simply made his own elusive statement by keeping his body close to Clea's, his arm curved around her shoulders.

Tonight they were a couple in all senses of the word, and Clea felt happy, too at peace to question its tenuous links.

All she knew was that she needed this—him. She had surrendered to her own yearnings, and Max seemed to be glad that she had. If guilt drove him, or that overactive sense of responsibility, then she wasn't going to question it just now.

Pregnancy had made her vulnerable, and Max seemed to like her dependency on him. Their desire for each other seemed to be enough to hold them together and, for now, that was all that mattered.

The evening dusk gave way to darkness, and the pretty lanterns were allowed to give the performance they were there for. The smell of juicy steaks teased the taste-buds, and the music drew them towards the dance-floor.

'Dance with me.' Max bent to murmur close to her ear while she was talking to one of her mother's friends.

She turned her face up to his, reading the dark glint in his eyes and smiling softly at it. 'Yes, please,' she replied.

There was something a little magical about them tonight. Max could feel it too, she knew, and as he drew her on to the dance-floor in Amy's drawing-room Clea stepped very close to him, so her body brushed his with an intimacy that held them breathless.

Her arms went beneath his jacket, stroking along his lean waist to the lithe curve of his back, and Max let out a soft breath that sighed a little as it was released, his hands splayed across her spine, holding her to the drugging warmth of his body.

The music swirled around them. Clea rested her cheek against his shoulder, and he responded by lowering his mouth to her hair. 'I wish we were alone,' he murmured deeply. 'It sets me on fire just to touch you.'

I know, thought Clea. You do the same for me. If only I lit other feelings in you. If only . . .

She turned her head so her mouth made moist contact with his warm throat, tongue flicking out to taste him with a sensuality she could not deny. Her fingers curled, nails digging into the hard muscled skin beneath the silk of his shirt, and Max jerked on a spasm of pleasure.

'Stop it,' he protested huskily. And Clea smiled when she felt the answering throb in his lower body press closer to her.

'You wanted to dance,' she reminded him throatily.

His hold on her tightened. 'It was either endure this torment, or drag you off to that bed your parents have kindly loaned us for tonight.'

'Poor Max!' she teased. 'Having to deny himself for the sake of boring convention.'

He gave a wry laugh. 'To think that I assured your doctor that *I* wouldn't overtire *you!*'

'Making love with you doesn't tire me,' she argued softly. 'It—it uplifts me. I love your body, Max,' she whispered to him in blatant seduction. 'All hard and fierce and . . .'

'Clea!' he warned roughly. 'Behave! Or I'll have to put the width of the room between us!' And he wasn't joking, Clea noted on a chuckle.

They did become separated later. Joe came looking for Max, dragging him off to meet someone who had voiced an interest in buying a computer system for his company.

The air had grown hot and sticky inside, so Clea wandered outside, breathing in the cooler evening air, glad of some time to herself. She walked slowly down the garden, smiling at the small clutches of people she passed by, following a line of pretty, coloured lanterns until she reached the darker end of the garden where the bench seat stood beneath the flowering cherry tree which was just beginning to sprout fruit. She sat down, relaxing back to enjoy the tranquillity. The music barely infiltrated this far down the garden; it was darker, the party seeming miles away from this secret hide-out she'd found for herself.

Her mind slipped back to the last time she had sat here, one cold and frosty morning four months ago, when James had put her through the third degree. She smiled at the memory. James had been so shocked, so absolutely floored by her news! Then he had laughed, she remembered. He had sat here, next to her, and guffawed like a man demented.

'Fancy meeting you here.' It was quite uncanny, having James's voice break into her thoughts like that when she had just been thinking about him. She looked up and smiled.

'You have fairies at the bottom of your garden, James,' she told him with mock solemnity, patting the seat beside her in invitation.

'Black-haired wicked sprites, you mean,' he drawled, taking the proffered seat.

'Were you looking for me?' She hoped not. It was nice here, she didn't feel ready to leave as yet.

'Mmm, yes and no,' he drawled evasively. 'Max was looking for you. Amy thought she'd seen you strolling this way, but couldn't be sure, so I suggested I come and look while Max searched the rooms inside the house.'

'All this concern!' she quipped. 'You'll have my head swelling, if you're not careful.'

James leaned back, his gaze on the swaying lanterns just beyond their hiding place. 'Don't you think our concern is justified?' he said after a moment.

Clea glanced sharply at him. He sounded grim, disparaging almost. 'I'm a very sensible person, James,' she claimed levelly. 'I wouldn't have come down here if I had been feeling in any way unwell.'

'I'm not talking about your physical condition.' He caught her gaze with a sharp one of his own. 'Why did you let Amy and I believe that Max felt nothing for you?' he asked suddenly, and Clea stiffened.

Then her mouth twisted wryly. 'Has he been using that

devastating charm of his to convert you, James?'

'That was not an answer to my question,' he drawled, refusing to be diverted.

'Ah!' she sighed. 'The question being, "Did I lie?" No,' she continued with the answer, 'I did not lie. Which leads to the next obvious question, as to whether Max has been misleading you. The answer to that is no, also. Max, you see, believes he cares for me, which is a long way from the actuality . . . Believing and being are two completely different things.'

'I like him,' James announced after a moment's thought.

'Amy does, too,' Clea pointed out sardonically. 'She already treats him like her son-in-law.' That mobile mouth went awry again. 'Poor Mother, she hates untidy ends. Max does, too. They're quite alike when I come to think about it.'

'Why are you living with him when you feel so much contempt for the man?' James challenged the bitterness he'd heard in her voice, and incorrectly interpreted.

Her head swung around to face him again. 'I don't hate Max!' she denied. 'I can't say I like him very much—not the old Max, anyway . . .' She frowned at her own confusion. 'But I don't hate him. I just won't marry him. that's all.'

'Why?'

She blinked. 'Why?' she repeated. 'Because he doesn't love me, that's why. You know that, James,' she went on impatiently. 'I explained it all to you very clearly, here, in this very same spot.'

'And the baby—what do you think his feelings are about the baby?'

Her face softened at that. 'Oh, he already loves the baby,' she said, with a certainty that came from deep within her. Her experience of his gentle care with her body when he made love to her, the way he would pay homage to the unborn child they had both made—they proved it without a doubt.

'I think you're being unfairly cruel to him.'

'What——?'

'In your efforts to make him pay for not loving you, you are deliberately denying him the right to give the child his name. That, to me, is both cruel and unnaturally selfish of you, Clea,' he judged. 'You seem quite prepared to let him care for you and the baby. You'll live with him as a married couple would live. Yet you deny him that one important thing that could make everything decent and right. And all for what, Clea?' he pressed on ruthlessly. 'Revenge? Jealousy, maybe—because he loves the baby more than he loves you?'

'James!' She jumped to her feet, her face flushed, breasts heaving with shock and distress that he could actually be saying these things to her. 'How could you use such terrible words to me? How could you . . .'

James remained calm, his eyes steady on her horrified face. 'Envy, resentment, jealousy and revenge, Clea,' he listed cruelly. 'Think about them. And, when you have, come to me and tell me—honestly—that your reasons for denying Max his right as the father of your child are purely altruistic, and that those reasons can stand up strongly against marrying and removing that *bastard* status you're determined to inflict on that baby!'

'That's enough!' grated a harsh voice. And it wasn't Clea's. Hers was locked in her throat, utterly trapped by the shock of James's attack.

Max's arm came protectively around her shoulders. His body was stiff with rage. He glared coldly down at an impervious James.

'None of this is any of your business!' Max's voice was like ice, cutting through the warm night, while Clea trembled violently in his embrace, her mind rocked with a culmination of overwrought emotion. Thoughts, feelings, James's ruthless accusations—all ran together and clashed, winging her off into a waking nightmare.

'Amy is my business,' James pointed out with amazing calm. 'And so, indirectly, is anything that affects my wife. Clea's situation affects her. So do you, come to that, Max.'

'I won't say this twice, so listen.' Max's face was like hewn rock, anger vibrating from every pore. 'If, as you say, Amy is your prime concern, then understand this—if you so much as mention our relationship again to Clea, I'll stop her from seeing either of you again—and think what that will do to your precious Amy!'

'Max . . .' Clea found enough control to speak, her hand pressing urgently to his heaving chest in appeal. She wasn't sure just how much of the conversation Max had overheard, but his furious reaction made her fear the worst. 'What James was saying isn't true! I——'

The hard arms around her tightened jerkily. 'Shut up, Clea!' he grated harshly.

She turned to face him fully, fear that James may have caused that dreaded break in the tenuous links she and Max had forged this past week making her clutch at his shirt, eyes bright with pained appeal.

'I love you, Max!' she cried in desperation. 'I love you! That's why I wouldn't tie you to me—not for anything in the world could I do that to you! Not for any of the reasons James was giving! I love you! I just couldn't . . .'

'Oh, Lord!' Max choked, and Clea began to cry quietly into his shoulder.

'And there——' drawled an outwardly unaffected James as he got up languidly from the bench seat '—is where I rest my case.' And he strolled off, leaving Clea and Max alone in the darkness, their bodies locked in a mutual agony of their own making.

'Clea,' Max whispered hoarsely.

'Take me home, Max,' she sobbed. 'I don't want to be here any more. Please, take me home.'

'No, wait,' he appealed, holding her closely to him. 'Wait!' he repeated roughly. He was trembling as badly as she. Clea clutched desperately at him still, so afraid that she couldn't think properly. Everything had been so beautiful! And now it was going all wrong!

'Max, please——!'

'Don't, Clea,' he groaned. 'Don't upset yourself like this!' Max took in a deep breath and let it out again slowly, grappling for self-control. 'Come and sit down and we'll . . .'

Clea shook her head. She didn't want to sit down, she didn't want to lose contact with the haven of his body and arms. Her grip on him intensified, and Max sighed softly.

'I have something I want to say to you,' he declared. 'But I'm afraid you're going to make yourself ill again if you don't calm yourself. Clea——' he appealed huskily. 'Won't you just sit down?' He tried to look into her face, but she wasn't letting him, burying herself deeper into his shirt front, shaking her head a second time in refusal.

'Don't let go of me,' she pleaded hoarsely.

His arms tightened. 'Never!' he vowed. 'Never again, Clea. I don't think I would survive it . . . Do you remember the first time we saw each other?' he murmured after a moment. 'Through the glass partitioning of the typing pool?' His cheek was warm on hers, his body cocooning hers in a tender embrace, his voice a comforting rumble in his hard chest. 'It was like being hit by a steam train,' he confessed wryly, and Clea nodded, because she had felt exactly the same. 'Like a fool, I tried dismissing you from my mind,' he went on grimly. 'I had an unbroken rule never to associate with my female staff;

it invariably led to complications and it seemed easier to ignore their—undeniable charms.' He laughed shortly, aware of how conceited he sounded. Then the grimness was back, and he sighed heavily. 'But not you, Clea—never you! I couldn't dismiss you from my mind. You remained there, like a phantom, clinging to the periphery of my consciousness, until I could stand it no longer, and made you my secretary. I decided—again with that conceit—that I only wanted to have you around so I could look at you, brighten up my day with a vision of a black-haired nymph with pansy eyes and a body that ignited the senses just to look at it. It took a month for my defences to topple,' he recalled wryly. 'Then I was plotting your seduction with a single-mindedness that shocked even me! We make beautiful love, Clea,' he murmured against her soft cheek. 'But I had that rule I disliked breaking, so I developed this clever dual role of lover and employer and I played it to its extreme, despite knowing I was being unfair to you.'

'I understood,' she whispered.

'I know you did, darling,' he replied grimly. 'But I don't want you to condone my behaviour. I was very cruel to you.'

Yes, Clea thought. He had been cruel, but she'd allowed him to be. She had been so infatuated with him then that he could do nothing wrong in her eyes.

'I had a whole week to acknowledge my faults when I went down to Devon. You'd changed towards me, and in my conceit I couldn't work out the reason why. My week of soul-searching left me feeling pretty grim with myself, I can tell you. I realised later, of course, that your withdrawal before I went away was because of the baby . . .'

'And Dianne Stone,' she put in huskily. 'Finding out about her hurt far more than learning about the baby.'

'Dianne Stone was nothing,' Max dismissed roughly. 'I was a fool on the run, and I used her, quite ruthlessly, to try to put a check on my growing feelings for you. To be frank, they terrified me. The last thing I wanted was to tie myself down. You were quite right when you said that to me. But I never touched her—haven't touched any other woman with any intimacy since you. I don't even want them—which was a shock to my system, I have to admit. I'd already begun to realise that things couldn't continue as they had been doing. That my feelings for you were far more involved than I believed—or wanted to believe,' he admitted ruefully. 'So I spent the week brooding, driving my mother up the wall with my black moods, and came back with all my decisions made and ready to magnanimously put them into immediate practice, to find you'd left the company! You have no idea what that did to me!' He groaned, pulling her closer. 'I was so angry, so frightened by what it meant, that I was building walls against you before I even saw you! So when you hit me with your news I reacted true to my conceit, and lashed out at you, and in the process burned all my own bridges where you were concerned.'

Clea was very still in the warm protection of his arms, trying to stop her hungry heart from reading too much into what he was saying. Yet all the clues were there, just begging to be correctly interpreted.

'I love you, Clea,' he admitted huskily, his voice low-pitched and deeply anxious. 'I loved you before I went to Devon. I loved you on sight, I think,' he ruefully added. 'I came back from Devon with the single purpose of putting our relationship on a firmer footing, then failed the ultimate test of my so-called love at the first hurdle . . . I've spent the ensuing months trying to make amends for that error. I hoped I was succeeding?' The question in his tone revealed his uncertainty. 'Your suggesting you live with me was meant to scare me off, I know that.'

Clea laughed huskily into his shirt, and Max dropped a smiling kiss on the top of her bowed head for it. 'But you had no idea how unwittingly you'd played into my hands. I'd been considering suggesting the same thing myself, but couldn't work up the courage to ask—you're a terrifying lady when your tongue gets started, Clea Maddon,' he teased softly. 'I wondered sometimes just what was hitting me when you started your character assassinations.'

'I was hurting.'

'I know,' he soothed. 'And I deserved it. I have been hoping that your coming to live with me would be a natural step towards the kind of permanent relationship I really want for us. I was willing to be patient, wait until you were ready to believe me when I admitted loving you. Tonight James has forced me into reviewing my plans somewhat, but the sincerity is still true. I want us to get married, as soon as we can, and not only for the baby's sake, but mine also, because I want to tie you to me before I go quietly out of my mind.'

James turned to look back into the shadows of his lanterned garden, picking out the two closely entwined figures, deep in serious conversation. And he sent a silent prayer up to the heavens that his ploy had worked. Clea had needed waking up from her stubborn blindness to Max. It had taken just one look at Max Latham, the day they had first met, for both himself and Amy to realise just what Max's feelings for Clea were. It made him want to kick himself for not forcing a meeting sooner, then maybe the unsatisfactory situation would not have gone on so long unresolved.

He turned, going in search of his wife to warn her of what he had done, and to expect a little hostility from her future son-in-law when they next saw him . . .

'Let's go home, Max,' Clea said softly, leaning feebly

against him, 'I don't want to be here any more. I want to be alone with you. I want to go home.'

'Home,' he sighed. 'Have you any idea how wonderful that sounds to me? Clea?' He groaned, pulling her closer.

She lifted her face at last, daring to search those urgent blue eyes for the sincerity she'd heard in his voice, and found it, blazing down on her with no cloaks to hide behind.

'I love you, Clea. Will you marry me, please?'

A sob rose in her throat, and she swallowed it down, smiling shakily at him, eyes bright with happy tears. 'Oh, Max!' she choked, and his chest heaved on an unsteady sigh. Then they were kissing fiercely, the need so dire that it held them lost in each other for a long time. The darkness at the bottom of Amy's garden, the pretty lanterns swinging gently from the trees just beyond, a perfect setting for their silent pledge.

'You haven't answered me,' Max murmured as their mouths broke apart reluctantly.

'About marrying you, you mean?' she teased, but softly, and with no cruelty. She kissed him on the mouth, just a gentle, loving kiss that said so much. 'Yes, please, Max. Oh, yes, please!'

Max wandered back into the bedroom with a cream towel slung low on his hips. He was rubbing his wet head with another towel.

'Come on, Clea!' he muttered. 'We'll be late if you don't get up and get ready!' Clea yawned and stretched lazily in the rumpled bed, a smile widening her generous mouth as a feeling of *déjà vu* swept over her.

'I like it here.'

Max grinned, one of his white-toothed, devastating smiles that rippled her heart. 'I know you do,' he said wickedly. 'But we're supposed to be getting married in an hour, and I don't think you, in your condition, can afford to be late!'

'Better late than never!' claimed the caustic Mrs Margaret Latham as she kissed Clea's cheek in congratulation an hour and a half later. 'I never thought my son slow on the uptake, but popping the question he had warned me about a whole four months before it happened is slow in anyone's books!' she glibly announced, then walked away, leaving Clea with her mouth hanging open in mute amazement.

'Your mother is crazy!' she said to Max later, when they stood in their apartment, alone at last. 'She actually had the cheek to imply that you informed her about your intention to marry me on your trip down to Devon!'

Max looked gravely at her astounded face, and said nothing. Clea blinked. 'It was true?' she gasped.

He nodded slowly.

'Oh, Max!' she said. 'What a pair of absolute idiots we've been!'

'Amen to that,' murmured Max, and drew her to him.

'Clea——?' Max leaned over her sleeping form, smiling indulgently to himself at the room she now took up in their bed.

She turned on to her back, reluctantly opening her eyes to squint up at his attractive face.

'James has just rung,' he informed her softly. 'I'm afraid your mother has beaten you to the winning post.'

'What?' She shot upright in the bed, blinking like an owl. 'You mean my mother——?' A hand went dramatically to her brow. 'What time is it? When did she start in labour? How is she? I have to get up!'

'It's five o'clock in the morning,' Max told her

patiently. 'Amy went into labour two hours ago. And she's doing fine. Easy, darling!' he warned as she hauled her heavily pregnant frame to the edge of the bed.

'I must go to the hospital,' she muttered, excitement and an odd panic making her feel confused. She stood up, swaying slightly, so Max had to steady her with a hand on her arm. 'I want to be there when she gives birth. I want to—aah!' she cried, as a sharp pain lanced through her lower body, arching her back in protest, sending her head flying back in a teeth-clenching reaction.

'Oh, hell!' groaned Max, catching her to him. 'Why in heaven's name did it have to choose now?'

Master James Laverne Junior was born just twenty-five minutes before his nephew Master Dominic Latham. Both babies were healthy and well—like their mothers.

'I love you, Clea,' Max whispered later. He was sitting beside the bed, searching her exhausted face with a mixture of deep pride and tender concern. 'I love our son. Thank you for him.'

'Think nothing of it,' she teased, smiling sleepily into his face, which still showed the strain witnessing their son's birth had placed on him. 'Poor Max,' she murmured softly. 'I think you suffered more than I did.'

'It was the sheer impotency I felt that hurt the most.'

'I can't see how you can claim impotency when I have actual proof of the opposite!' Clea argued, tongue in cheek, deliberately misinterpreting his meaning.

Max gave a rueful shake of his head. 'Still able to find the clever remark, even when half-asleep, Clea!'

'I may bore you otherwise,' she teased.

'Oh, never boring, darling,' Max denied huskily. 'I

count my blessings every single day since we married. I haven't felt one regret.'

'Good,' she said, and fell asleep with a serene smile about her mouth that made Max have to kiss it.

'It's a good job one of them is blond and the other dark-haired,' James remarked about the two baby boys the next day, when he came to visit Clea. 'Because they both possess a matching pair of purple eyes that will drive the ladies wild when they grow up.'

'Rakes!' Clea instantly predicted. 'Just like their disreputable papas! It'll be bred into them, you mark my words. They'll pattern themselves on their lecherous daddies, and cause mayhem wherever they go!'

'You mean us?' chimed two aggrieved voices.

'Models of respectability, we are,' Max pronounced innocently.

'Hah!' said Clea.

Harlequin Temptation dares to be different!

Once in a while, we Temptation editors spot a romance that's truly innovative. To make sure *you* don't miss any one of these outstanding selections, we'll mark them for you.

When the "Editors' Choice" fold-back appears on a Temptation cover, you'll know we've found that extra-special page-turner!

THE

Temptation

EDITORS

Harlequin Presents

Coming Next Month

Available in February wherever paperback books are sold, or through Harlequin Reader Service:

In the U.S.
901 Fuhrmann Blvd.
P.O. Box 1397
Buffalo, N.Y. 14240-1397

In Canada
P.O. Box 603
Fort Erie, Ontario
L2A 5X3